the proper *princess*

Her Royal Duty, Book Four

MELISSA McCLONE

Cardinal Press, LLC
August 2019
ISBN-13: 9781944777340

Dedication

To everyone who wants a happily ever after!

Chapter One

In her bedroom, Princess Madeleine-Victoria of Gaullia stared at the gown hanging from the top of the armoire. Yards of luscious white fabric decorated with the finest lace appliques, crystal accents, and intricate stitching fell to the floor where the cathedral train pooled. The wedding dress was meant to be worn by a princess bride and future queen.

A crown-jewel-sized lump lodged in her throat.

That would be her.

Which was the problem.

She should be ecstatic to see the magnificent dress

designed specifically for her. The craftsmanship astonished her. Each detail was exact. Much of which had been created by hand.

Any other bride would be thrilled to wear this gown but not her. Dread knotted her stomach. The thought of putting on the dress made her skin itch. Not the reaction a bride-to-be should have, but she couldn't help herself.

Madeleine sighed, a long exhale capable of powering the windmills dotting her country's plains.

Pull yourself together.

This wasn't how a princess should behave.

For the past five years, she'd known and accepted that a loveless, arranged marriage would be her fate. Her parents hadn't been in a rush to find her a husband after Louie, her fiancé, died. They'd allowed her to do as she wished, which had meant getting a graduate degree in political science while seeing to her royal obligations. Not once had she contemplated not doing her duty.

Until now.

She reached out to touch the exquisite fabric before pressing her arm to her side.

Could she turn her back to the expectations placed on her and say no? Especially when her parents and brother—her entire country—were counting on her.

Not because they wanted a royal wedding. The stakes were higher than that. This was to save her kingdom and her people.

Yes, she had a choice, but did she want to risk the land where she'd been born and raised?

No.

The answer was as simple as that but led to a quagmire of complicated emotions.

With her heart sinking, she stared at the gorgeous wedding gown. She might have a choice—her father was a king not a dictator—but the consequences were too great if she chose to go against her parents' wishes.

Maybe *he* won't be as horrible as she'd heard.

"He" being her intended husband.

Crown Prince Enrique Cierzo de Amanecer from La Isla de la Aurora, the island of the dawn.

She'd never met him, only seen his picture. He was attractive, but he'd been called selfish and self-centered by the few women he'd dated. A surprisingly low number of dates. Not one serious relationship had been mentioned in the articles she'd read. He was said to have issues, most particularly wanting to be catered to by those around him. She wished they had time to date so she could find out what he was like because he sounded like a complete narcissist. Granted, he wasn't the only prince like that.

She also knew that the media exaggerated and lied. Gossip and rumors were part of being a royal, except not one article had mentioned wild parties or a revolving bedroom door. The criticism centered on Enrique's personality, which made him seem less than desirable as a spouse. Not only that, but it also appeared as if his search for a bride had been met with only disastrous results. His once-fiancée, the wealthy and beautiful Princess Julianna of Aliestle, had canceled their engagement and married his younger brother.

How had that happened?

And why?

Julianna would have been queen if she'd married the older brother. The fact she hadn't suggested Prince Enrique must be the definition of awful.

Madeleine shuddered. If only one of the other eligible male royals on the continent was to be her intended spouse. But the crown prince of La Isla de la Aurora had something the others didn't. Still…

"I'm cursed."

Logical or not, that was the only explanation.

Feeling this way was nothing new.

Once upon a time with another groom and a different gown, she'd been floating off the ground, unable to sleep or eat, due to the anticipation of marrying her one true love. If only…

She went to her nightstand where a bouquet—a gift from Enrique—sat. The blossoms scented the air with a sweet fragrance, but she ignored that.

Madeleine opened the narrow top drawer and removed a framed photograph.

Louis.

Her Louie.

The love of her life.

Her fiancé.

The man she wanted to be the father of her children.

"If only you were still here with me, my love."

Even though she'd memorized every detail about Crown Prince Louis Fredrick, she stared at the photo. Strands of his long blond hair blew in the wind. His vibrant blue eyes had been able to see beyond the surface, knowing what was in her heart often before she did. Those soft lips had kissed her for the first time when she'd been a teenager and for the last time when she was twenty-two, days before they were to marry.

"I wish you could tell me everything will be okay."

With her fingertip, Madeleine touched the glass covering his picture. The pang in her heart was as familiar as taking a breath. So was the slight burn in her eyes. She wiped away the tears before they ruined her makeup.

Five years hadn't diminished the heartache of losing Louie in a helicopter crash. The suddenness of the tragedy had sent her world spinning. The fact she was supposed to have been with him compounded the loss with overwhelming guilt. Her parents had brought in a grief counselor to help her muddle through.

Overall, Madeleine supposed she was doing better. The passage of time had made her sorrow not as visible on the outside. She could smile and pretend all was well. Everyone had been fooled.

But nothing, including the passing of years, would lessen her love.

Madeleine pulled the necklace she wore from

under her clothing. A ring hung from the long gold chain—Louie's crest. She'd returned her engagement ring because it was a family heirloom, part of their royal collection. But his parents had given her Louie's signet ring, the one he'd worn on his pinkie, though he'd left it at home the day of the crash.

A knock sounded on the door.

She placed the photo into the drawer before blinking to make sure no more tears welled. "You may enter."

Her maid, Lilia, bustled into the room. In her early-thirties, she wore a plain black dress with a white apron. Her hair was pulled back into a tight bun. The severe look did nothing to let the world—at least the one inside the castle walls—see the vibrant, kind woman who had kept Madeleine going when she hadn't wanted to get out of bed or eat.

As Lilia studied the gown, an expression of awe appeared on her face. "It is a lovely wedding dress, ma'am."

Was Lilia remembering the other wedding dress a younger Madeleine had only worn for the fittings?

Best not to go there.

"Yes, the dress designer outdid herself." Somewhat surprising given Madeleine's only request had been a design different from her first wedding dress. She only wished she felt an ounce of joy at the thought of wearing this new one.

She turned away from the gown. "Has our visitor

arrived?"

"Not yet, ma'am. The crown prince should arrive in an hour or two."

The weight of the country on Madeleine's shoulders lifted. Air flowed freely into her lungs. She had a reprieve, if only for a short time before they would sit together to have afternoon tea.

Eyes clouding with concern, Lilia took a step closer. "Ma'am?"

Madeleine held up her hand. "I'm fine."

As fine as she would be with only half a heart beating in her chest. Louie had taken the other half with him when he died. Somehow she'd survived this long, but she wasn't sure how.

"A little tired." She didn't want to take her frustrations out on Lilia.

"I doubt you've been sleeping well with so much going on." Lilia gave her an encouraging smile. "Meeting the man you will marry must be so exciting."

Madeleine's blood turned ice-cold. "You have no idea."

Another knock sounded.

What was this? An impromptu soiree? She thought that wouldn't happen until their guest arrived for afternoon tea. "Enter."

Her mother, Queen Anne-Elizabeth, came into the room with quick, purposeful steps. Nothing about the woman was soft and genteel, except the scent of her expensive perfume. The royal bloodlines flowing through her veins meant she was related to many of the names listed in Burke's Peerage. The queen would put Mother Nature into her place, if need be.

She studied the gown with the eyes of a fashion icon. "The dress came out better than I expected given the rush. You will be a stunning bride."

As a knot formed in Madeleine's stomach, she forced a smile. "Thank you, ma'am."

"Are you ready for this afternoon?" her mother asked.

A proper princess could give only one response. "Yes, ma'am."

"Excellent, my dear." Her mother's gaze ran the length of the gown again. "Your father would like a word with you in his office."

The last thing Madeleine wanted was for her father to worry about her or anything else. He'd done enough of that these past months. "I will go now, Mother."

Before she lost her courage and called off the wedding.

Stop.

She almost heard Louie telling her not to be such a drama princess. That she was overreacting.

Oh, how she hoped her love was correct.

Downstairs, her father's assistant, Edward, an older man with short gray hair and beady eyes masked by wire-rimmed glasses, opened the door to the king's office. "He is expecting you, ma'am."

"Thank you, Edward." Her insides trembled, but

she strode inside. Royals weren't supposed to show emotion in public. Her family frowned upon doing that in private, also. She'd learned from an early age, the shower was the only place to cry.

Her father, King Leon-Maximilian, stood in his office. He was an imposing man, over six feet tall and barrel-chested, who intimidated most people. He didn't frighten her or her brother, Karl, because the king was a giant teddy bear with them. But neither had ever wanted to disappoint their father…their king. So far, they hadn't.

She pushed back her shoulders and raised her chin. "You asked to see me, sir."

"Your fiancé will arrive shortly."

Even though she'd never met Enrique and the marriage contract had yet to be signed, no one else thought calling the man her fiancé was odd. Still, she nodded.

"The crown prince will make a fine king. He's a skilled negotiator. In the past year, he and his younger brother, Alejandro, have made dramatic improvements to their country's economy."

Madeleine dug her manicured fingernails into her palms. She didn't want to be reminded why Enrique would be a wonderful husband for her. "Father, I know the reasons I'm marrying Enrique, and they have nothing to do with the prince's statesmanship or his finance acumen. We need to become allies of Aliestle to save the land near our border."

Because of that country's abundance of rare natural resources, King Alaric had the money to do as he pleased. He'd decided expanding his borders was his next pet project, and he was using loans made to Gaullia's treasury to achieve his goal. Loans that wouldn't have been necessary had Louie lived and married her.

Her father nodded. "Since Princess Julianna married Enrique's younger brother, an alliance has been forged between the two kingdoms. Not as strong as I hoped because of the princess's disobedience to her father's wishes, but Alaric attended her wedding a year ago, which is more than anyone expected."

"His generous wedding gift to the couple would pay off much of our country's debt." She'd been researching options to help her country without having to marry, but she'd found none. Unfortunately. "If we become a part of that alliance, King Alaric will reconsider demanding our land in lieu of payment. Even if I didn't have a master's degree in political science, I would understand the stakes."

Her father's shoulders sagged. "This is not the match you hoped for."

"Louie was the only husband I wanted," Madeleine said in a matter-of-fact tone. Her one true love was dead. She never would love again. "But I was raised to do my duty for Gaullia, and I shall. I won't fail you, Mother, Karl, or our country."

That was what her father expected to hear, what

over a quarter century of etiquette and protocol training had taught her to say. Yet…

Her heart wanted to scream—to rebel.

If Louie hadn't died, her life would be the definition of happy, overflowing with love and joy. They would be married with children—a crown prince or princess of their own. Maybe two.

She bit the inside of her cheek to regain her focus.

Her father's gaze softened. The lines on his face relaxed. "You've always been a proper princess, a living example to the youth of what duty and dedication mean. I pray that will help you in your marriage and the future."

His voice wasn't as strong as usual. A hint of fear laced each word. She'd never seen him like this, and that worried her. Karl was twenty-nine, two years older than her, but he wasn't ready to be king. He needed time to learn, grow, and…mature.

"It shall, Father." Madeleine had the feeling until the wedding vows were exchanged in the cathedral and the royal union official, her father wouldn't relax. "Is there anything else you need?"

He started to speak but then stopped himself. "Not now."

She curtsied before turning to leave.

"Mads…"

Her father rarely used her childhood nickname. Only Karl called her that now.

She glanced over her shoulder. "Yes, sir?"

"If the crown prince is awful—"

"I'm sure he isn't that bad." She said the words for both their sakes. "People exaggerate. Especially about royals. It will work out."

"Thank you, my dear." Her father sank onto one of the sofas. The dark circles and bags under his eyes became clearer. "Gaullia needs this royal marriage to survive, but I want you to be happy."

"I shall be fine." Not happy, however. That wasn't possible without Louie in her life. "Don't worry about me, Father."

With that, she left his office, hurrying past the security guards stationed outside the door and Edward's neat and tidy desk.

People exaggerate.

She hoped that was the case with Crown Prince Enrique. Because the alternative…

No, she wouldn't think about it.

Chapter Two

Crown Prince Enrique Cierzo de Amanecer stood in the king's office. He was set to depart the palace in fifteen minutes, but his father had asked to see him, so here he was.

Enrique flicked a piece of lint from his sleeve. His tailored suit fit perfectly, but the silk tie around his neck seemed to tighten like a noose. Even though he wanted to loosen the knot, he kept his arms pressed against his sides. Appearing weak or nervous would only make matters worse.

"Do you understand what's at stake, my son?" His

father's voice was firm yet filled with compassion. An odd mixture, but not an unexpected one. Over the past two years, King Dario of La Isla de la Aurora had strived to be a better father to his two sons, which was why Enrique hated the position they found themselves in.

"I do, sir." He only hoped his princess bride was willing to say "I do" to him.

"I'm sorry, Enrique."

His father's heartfelt apologies for the way he'd treated both his sons had helped them become a family again. But this time, the words were unnecessary. "You don't owe me or anyone else an apology, sir."

"I feel as if I do." As his father paced the length of his office, his shoulders hunched in a not-so-kingly manner. The man could no longer carry the weight of his country's demands, which was why his doctors suggested he retire. "I had no idea when I announced my abdication date, the Parliament would change the succession law. I still can't believe they are requiring the crown prince to be married before he can ascend the throne. It's ridiculous and unheard of. I have asked—demanded—they relent, to no avail. I may still wear the crown, but my hands are tied."

The remorse in his father's voice matched his expression. Each passing month aged his father more. He needed to be on the golf course enjoying his golden years, not battling politicians with agendas.

"I don't blame you for anything, sir." Enrique

didn't. He'd been trying not to take Parliament's declaration personally. Yes, he'd exploded in private but not in public. That was…progress. "I disagree with Parliament's change, but I see why they did so."

His younger brother, Alejandro, was married to Jules, AKA Princess Julianna of Aliestle, an obscenely wealthy albeit tiny European country. They'd recently celebrated their one-year anniversary. She was to have been Enrique's bride—and, if she'd married him as planned, none of this would be an issue—but she'd fallen for his brother. Even if Enrique might lose the one thing he'd ever wanted, he was happy for the deliriously in-love couple.

"Parliament wants what they believe will be best for our kingdom—to strengthen our alliance with Jules's father," Enrique continued. "King Alaric wants nothing more than for his only daughter to be queen. If that happens, our island will reap the rewards and prosper."

"True, but I believe more is behind the change," his father admitted. "Before you were born, Parliament tried to kill the monarchy so they could control everything. I fear the same mentality has taken hold of those robed fools. But I must give them credit. Setting ridiculous ascension laws is less messy than a coup would be."

Heat rushed through Enrique's body. Muscles tensed. He gritted his teeth.

"The monarchy will not end." The words came out

short and clipped. Just the thought made Enrique's gut clench. "That will never happen."

His father's gaze narrowed. "You sound certain."

"I am." Enrique's plan was foolproof.

If they had to use it…

"Your brother doesn't want to be king." Regret filled his father's voice.

"That is true, but Alejandro has reconsidered thanks to his lovely wife. He understands what his royal duty is and has embraced it."

His father clutched the back of a chair. "Are you serious?"

Enrique nodded once, sending a slash of pain ripping through him. His father needed to know the plan, even if Enrique hoped not to need it. "If I…fail in Gaullia, I will relinquish my title as crown prince, and Alejandro will ascend the throne instead."

The lines on his father's forehead deepened. "Did you or Alejandro come up with this plan?"

"I did, but he agreed. As did Jules."

The actual discussion hadn't been as simple as it sounded. Even though his father had threatened to bypass Enrique in the line of succession if he didn't follow orders, he had spent his life preparing to be king. He'd turned himself into a clone of the king, much to the dismay of Alejandro. Enrique had finally realized that wasn't good for any of them. Still, it wasn't in his nature—though he'd been trying to change that—to be selfless. But the continuation of his family's rule was the most important thing. If worse came to worst, he would ensure that happening.

"Who else knows of your plan?" his father asked.

"Only the four of us." Enrique hadn't wanted to tell his father until Alejandro had committed himself one hundred percent to the plan. That happened last night. "No matter whether a royal wedding occurs in Gaullia, our family's rule over La Isla de la Aurora will continue."

Even if Enrique wouldn't be the one with the title and the crown.

As his stomach roiled, he forced himself to breathe.

Don't think about that.

His father's expression remained tense. "What about you?"

Enrique would have laughed, except he would likely appear a madman. Which he was. The quest to find a royal bride had been pure madness. His many failures to secure a match…

Pathetic.

But the blame was his. And his alone.

"I will be…fine." A lie, but what else could he say? His father's health had become a serious concern. "Don't worry about me."

"You are my son. I will worry, especially since you were raised to be—"

"King," Enrique finished for him. "Which is why I'll do everything in my power to see the monarchy remains."

Even without me.

Affection filled his father's eyes. "You have changed so much these past two years."

"I've been trying." With Alejandro and Jules's help.

"You're succeeding."

In some ways, yes. But not where it mattered most now.

Enrique's future rested in the hands of an unknown princess from an obscure country. He had been asked to go to Gaullia when protocol dictated she should come to him. Yet, he was going and agreed to be married there because she was his last chance to be king.

He prayed Princess Madeleine was more open to an arranged marriage than the other single princesses he'd met. A few hadn't allowed discussions about a match to occur. Others had met him once before rejecting him. Some spent a few days with him. One had banished him from her country when he'd unknowingly offended her.

Note to self: never mention a woman's calves.

He swallowed a sigh. "Let's hope I have one more success in me."

His father touched his shoulder. "No matter what happens, I am proud of the man you have become, my son."

A lump burned in Enrique's throat. He was thirty-five, but he wasn't used to such compliments from his father. That might be the last one he received, in person. Hearing "man" not "prince" or "ruler" was not lost on Enrique. No one believed he would return to the island with a bride.

Not even him.

Although Jules begged to differ, Enrique's mother had been correct when she'd left the island—and him—twenty-seven years ago. He might have been only eight, but he remembered what she'd told his father. Enrique's heart wasn't capable of loving. He was flawed when it came to personal relationships.

Broken.

His recent failures magnified his past ones and reaffirmed he was broken in a way that couldn't be fixed. But duty required him to try, no matter the odds, before he gave up everything that mattered to him.

"Thank you, sir." Enrique forced a smile. "I'll do my best not to disappoint you or our kingdom."

"I know you will." His father's gaze softened. "We shall see you at the final rehearsal."

Enrique wasn't the only one lying. Given his past record, he doubted he would make it as far as the day before the wedding, but he would play along. "I look forward to seeing you, Alejandro, and Jules in Gaullia."

"I love you." His father hugged him. "Safe travels, my son."

Until Jules entered their lives two years ago, hugs, compliments, and affection had been scarce at the palace, but his father had done a turnaround after seeing how poorly King Alaric treated Jules and her brother Brandt.

Enrique fought the unfamiliar urge to cling to his father. But he couldn't stand here forever. "I need to go to the airport."

As he left his father's office, Enrique didn't dare look back. If he did, he might want to stay. Instead, he kept his shoulders back and his chin up.

His footsteps echoed through the hallway. The limousine was waiting, but he was in no rush to leave the palace.

His…home.

In the foyer, uniformed attendants stood on either side of the heavy wooden doors. He acknowledged them with a nod before focusing on the marble statue of Eos, the Goddess of the Dawn and the Greek counterpart to the Roman Aurora, looming large in the palace's entryway.

Growing up, he'd believed Eos was there to watch over him because he was to be king. But he'd made too many mistakes to have had any kind of otherworldly guidance. Still, his hand touched the cold stone—a way to ground himself and to say…goodbye.

Because Enrique hadn't mentioned if he didn't wed, he wouldn't be returning to the island. The kingdom needed to embrace Alejandro, who would be their new crown prince, not have the former one hanging around like a specter of what might have been.

He'd packed three suitcases—two with clothes he

would need for his trip to Gaullia and a third with those items he didn't want to leave behind. Unfortunately, one thing he would have to live without was the palace garden. Nurturing the plants had been his escape since he was a child, and under his guidance, the garden flourished. More had been added over the years. The groundskeeper assured him the staff would tend the plants while he was away.

The thought of never working in his beloved garden or having the sweet fragrance of the blossoms tickle his nose again cut Enrique to the core. He'd grown up believing he was irreplaceable, but the garden would survive without him and so would the island. He didn't know if the realization left him humbled or devastated. But he had no time to dwell on it.

For better or for worse, he had a plane to catch.

Chapter Three

"The limousine is crossing the moat."

Madeleine understood Karl's excited tone. It wasn't, however, for the reason the staff assumed— meeting the man his sister would marry. No, her brother was relieved someone could save their country's land from being taken by Aliestle. Otherwise, there might not be much left of their kingdom for him to rule once he became king.

She straightened her skirt. Out of habit, not because she needed to fix anything. No one would allow her to appear less than perfect. Today more so than any other day.

"You look lovely, ma'am." Lilia gave her the once-over. "The crown prince will surely fall in love with you at first sight."

Madeleine shuddered. Love was the last thing she wanted. She'd lost the love of her life. There was never to be another. This royal union would be a state marriage. Dare she hope for separate bedrooms? Perhaps that would come after she gave birth to the required heir and spare.

Mrs. Hobbs, who oversaw the castle's staff and royal family, clapped. The sound echoed through the foyer. "Everyone out front and take your places as we practiced yesterday."

The uniformed staff members rushed outside. Choreographed chaos if there was such a thing.

Mrs. Hobbs motioned to Madeleine and her brother. "That includes you two. I'll get the staff situated then position you."

The woman had been doing that since Madeleine and Karl were little children.

Flexing his left hand, Karl, dressed in a suit and tie, exited first. He was two years older than her and her best friend. He'd stepped into that role after Louie died.

She followed her brother. The temperature was fifteen degrees hotter outside. Typical for August.

As Mrs. Hobbs spoke with the staff, Karl stopped on the steps. "Ready?"

Dread had been building for days. Madeleine didn't want to put off the meeting any longer. "Yes. I am."

Concern clouded his blue-eyed gaze. "I hope you sound more enthusiastic when you're introduced to your future husband or he might take offense."

Seriously? Her brother, too? She clenched her teeth. "I know what's expected of me."

"Then embrace your duty." He kept his voice low because of the guards behind them. "If you're fighting the situation or yourself, he will know."

"I'm trying." And she was.

"Try harder." Karl glanced at the approaching black limousine.

The Gaullian flag fluttered. For once, seeing the familiar royal blue, bright red, and white colors brought little comfort to Madeleine. She wasn't expecting Prince Charming, but she would settle for Prince Not-So-Bad.

"At least the crown prince came to Gaullia." Which wasn't the norm for an arranged royal marriage. Everyone she'd known in this situation had traveled to the groom's kingdom. "I'm thankful for that."

"Father's request. A deal-breaker from what I understand."

"Father said he wanted to make the introduction easier on me."

"Yes, but..." Karl's jaw tensed. "As long as Enrique is within our borders, King Alaric won't do anything...sketchy."

Her forehead throbbed. The weight on her shoulders quadrupled, but she forced herself to stand straight with proper princess posture. At least how her etiquette instructors defined it.

The staff formed two lines with a space in between them for their guest to pass on a red carpet.

The sun shone brightly in the cornflower blue sky. Not a wisp of clouds or breeze. A perfect August day. A good sign of things to come? She hoped so.

If only her emotions matched the weather. Instead, she was riding out a thunderstorm with gale force winds. She fought the urge to cling to her brother to keep from being blown away.

She realized two people were missing from the welcoming committee. "Where are Mother and Father?"

"They felt it best for us to greet Enrique without them, so he didn't feel overwhelmed. You'll take him directly to the tea."

Madeleine clutched his arm. "You're not going?"

"I wasn't invited." As Karl's expression softened, he patted her hand. "This is for the best, Mads. I'm here if you need me, but you must get used to doing more on your own. When you leave Gaullia—"

"I don't want to think about that."

She'd clung to Karl after Louie's death. Her brother had been grieving the loss of his longtime friend, too. He'd chosen Madeleine over his then-fiancée, which led to that princess canceling their engagement. He was still single because women were jealous of his close relationship to his sister.

"Promise you'll visit me," she added.

"Of course, I will." Karl winked. "I expect a room to be reserved at the palace for my use."

"If I have any say, it shall be done."

The limousine pulled onto the curved cobblestone drive in front of the castle.

She shivered.

Karl squeezed her hand. "It will be okay."

Okay. Okay. Okay.

If she kept telling herself that, she might come to believe it.

The limo stopped. A valet opened the rear passenger door.

No music played, but in her head, coronets sounded to announce the arrival.

Please let this go well.

"Well" meaning she could tolerate the crown prince's presence without getting sick to her stomach. Madeleine hoped she wasn't setting too high an expectation.

A middle-aged man exited first. He wore a suit, but she imagined he'd be more comfortable in fatigues. His athletic physique belied the gray in his black hair and the lines on his face. His watchful eyes surveyed each person before zeroing in on the castle guards standing on either side of the front door.

As if satisfied with the security, he leaned into the

limo before straightening.

A dark-haired man with olive skin slid out of the vehicle. His shoes gleamed as if recently polished. His tailored suit hadn't wrinkled during his flight. The blue in his silk tie matched the sky overhead. And his face…

Stunning.

Her breath caught in her throat.

Photographs hadn't done justice to Enrique's chiseled features and warm brown eyes. Or his almost black hair, which wasn't as short as his pictures, but longer with a wave and slight curls at the ends.

Tall, dark, and handsome.

If he wasn't a prince, he could easily be a model, both on the runway and in print. Having a piece of eye candy for a husband was something she should be happy about, right?

The female staff members preened as if to catch the prince's attention. As he greeted each one with a dazzling smile, Madeleine could almost hear ovaries exploding beneath the prim uniforms and crisp, white aprons. Even those who were older appeared taken in by the prince.

Relief flowed through Madeleine. The rumors of his lack of social skills appeared to be highly exaggerated. Thank goodness.

Mrs. Hobbs introduced them, using their full names and titles with a few hand flourishes thrown in for effect.

As dictated by protocol, Karl greeted their visitor

first. The two men exchanged handshakes and pleasantries before Enrique turned his attention to Madeleine.

His gaze met hers. Thick lashes framed his stunning eyes. Gold flecks glimmered in his amber-brown irises.

Her heart bumped.

The reaction surprised her. Bothered her, too.

She chalked it up to nerves.

Stepping closer, he raised her hand to his mouth. His skin was warm and rougher than she expected. He kissed the top. His lips lingered before he let go. "You have a lovely smile."

"Thank you." Except she hadn't been smiling.

Was he the type to give false flattery or had he seen a photograph of her smile? If the latter was true, did that make him a stalker or curious about her?

Madeleine didn't want to know the answer. "Welcome to Gaullia. We…I appreciate you making the trip to my home."

"Anything to make you happy." He stared at her for longer than was socially acceptable.

As flutters filled her stomach, she looked away. Instinct screamed to flee. Heaven knew she would if she could, but duty required she see this through. And not only this introduction, unfortunately.

"I've never been to Gaullia," Enrique continued. "I'm sure there's more to see besides the windmills and farmland your country is known for."

Karl's jaw tensed. He flashed her an *is-this-guy-for-real* glance.

Okay, Enrique's words could be taken as a slight, but they could be worse. He hadn't cursed or yelled or…

"Oh." The crown prince stiffened. A pensive expression crossed his face as if he were trying to remember something or maybe he'd realized how what he'd said might have sounded to her and Karl. "I like your shoes, Madeleine. Your outfit is…nice. And your…hair, too."

Karl snorted.

She swallowed a laugh because the compliments didn't sound sincere, especially since Enrique hadn't glanced at her feet once. The words were practiced—a list he'd memorized.

Still she kept smiling. Closemouthed. That was all she could manage. "Thank you."

He beamed. "You're welcome."

Weird, he appeared pleased with himself. Which made zero sense given his verbal lapses so far.

"I'm eager to get to know you," he added. "Given we'll be married and sharing a bed in less than two weeks, the sooner that happens, the better."

Her muscles tightened. Each of her nerve endings stiffened. She couldn't imagine kissing him, let alone…

Karl shot her a hard glare, one that told her to remain in control.

Madeleine was trying. She wanted to blame his

behavior on being nervous, but the gossip about his social skills appeared to be true. Yes, it—he—could be worse, but given what he'd said in the first minutes of meeting her, things would only go downhill from here.

"Let's go inside." Karl motioned to the castle's open doors. "I have business to attend to, but my parents are joining you and Madeleine for tea."

Even though he'd been excluded, Karl was gracious, but her brother was the definition of kind. He hated conflict, which was why he'd admitted to being relieved their father was king, not him, or Aliestle might have already seized their land.

Both men waited for Madeleine to enter the castle first.

"Follow me," she said, not glancing behind her.

Enrique quickly fell into step beside her. "The stone walls are authentic-looking, but it must cost a fortune to heat the castle in the winter."

Was he uncouth or clueless?

Not that one was better than the other.

She took a breath before exhaling slowly. "The stone walls are centuries old and covered with tapestries to maintain a consistent temperature inside. The castle has been renovated several times over the centuries." She paused, almost biting her tongue. "We even have indoor plumbing."

She shouldn't have mentioned the plumbing, but what he said annoyed her. They were a modern country, albeit small with agriculture as their main export, but they were as technologically advanced as others on the continent.

"Good to know the moat is only for show." Humor gleamed in his eyes.

She found zero amusement in what he said so she remained silent.

"As for the temperature, the weather in the Isla de la Aurora is not only consistent but what you find in vacation paradises." Enrique didn't seem to realize he annoyed her. "You'll enjoy living on the Mediterranean after growing up landlocked and having to deal with the harsh, cold winters here."

Could the man say anything without it being a putdown on something else?

She blew out a breath. "Your island sounds lovely."

"It rivals your beauty." He reached toward her face.

She flinched.

He lowered his hand. Swallowed. "Though with your fair skin, you'll want to slather on the sunscreen, especially in the summer."

Okay, his wanting to avoid her being sunburnt was kind and caring. That had to count for something, right?

"You don't want to end up wrinkled with sunspots," he added with a shudder.

Just shoot me now.

She glanced at Karl who seemed as bewildered by Enrique as she was. The man had no filter, or if he did, he needed a new one.

"Work calls. I'll leave you two," Karl blurted, as if wanting to make his escape. "Enjoy the tea."

With that, her brother headed toward his office.

"The sitting room is this way." Maybe her parents would have a better idea of how to deal with the crown prince because Madeleine was ready to send him on his way. She led Enrique under the arched doorway to the royal family's private wing.

The public rooms lay on the other side of the foyer and were only used for tours and state visitors. The biggest difference between the two sides wasn't the décor—both were elegantly appointed—but the warmth and comfort of the furniture and accessories on the family side. Framed photographs, landscapes painted by Karl, and embroidery she'd made hung on the walls.

Enrique stepped into the sitting room. "This is charming. So welcoming."

"Our family area is on this side of the castle. We…I thought this would be a more comfortable place for us to get acquainted."

That decision hadn't been for Enrique's benefit but hers. She'd wanted to see how he fit in with her family without the formality of the public rooms, but now she second-guessed herself, given the elaborate tea arrangement on the corner table. A three-tiered serving platter held canapes, triangular sandwiches, and desserts. A basket of scones with small bowls of clotted cream and jelly was next to a plate of sliced fruit and berries.

"I prefer the more casual atmosphere." He smiled at her. "We will be family soon enough."

A chill ran along her spine. She forced herself not to cross her arms over her chest. What he said was true, but that only ramped up her anxiety. "Planning a wedding to someone I never met has been a bit…nerve-racking. As is meeting you now."

The "bit" was an under-exaggeration. Madeleine wasn't sure why she'd admitted that. Although at this point, she assumed he'd formed his opinion—and not a good one—of their country full of windmills and farmlands and drafty old castles. Heaven only knew what he thought of her. Guess she would find out later today when they were scheduled to sign the marriage contract.

Madeleine would put her signature on the document for her country's sake. Would Enrique? She wasn't sure what to hope for. Although a part of her wished he wouldn't, despite what that would mean for Gaullia.

"The marriage negotiations and this visit have been completely nerve-racking for me, so I'm envious of your 'bit.'" Enrique's cheeks reddened before he stiffened. "I apologize. I shouldn't have admitted that."

"I'm glad you did." Knowing that made him appear more human and not a man who only spouted off faults. "I'm your fiancée so it's not a *faux pas*."

"Unlike some others I've made since arriving," he admitted to her surprise. "I'm sorry. Discussing business or politics comes easily. Social situations, however, are more difficult for me. I apologize for the past and any future mishaps. I assure you, there will be so many you will lose count."

His confession showed he was self-aware, but if that was the case, why didn't he think before he spoke?

"I appreciate the warning," she said.

For a minute, perhaps longer, they stood in silence. The distance seemed to widen the gap between them even though they stood only three feet apart.

Footsteps sounded.

Relief flooded her.

Mrs. Hobbs entered first, announcing her parents with lofty titles and more names than a normal human could remember. Madeleine only knew them because she'd been tested on them and punished if she made an error.

Her father shook Enrique's hand. "It's a pleasure to see you again, Enrique."

"The pleasure is all mine, sir." Enrique's smile was tight. He stood tall and proud but not at ease. "It's been a while since we met."

"That was two years ago at the summit meeting."

"Yes." Enrique's gaze traveled to her mother. "I'm looking forward to my stay in Gaullia."

"And the royal wedding, I hope." Her mother's voice sounded upbeat, but the lines on her face were deeper than usual.

"Of course." Enrique smiled at Madeleine. "That is the reason I am here. To finalize the marriage agreement, get to know my lovely bride, and once everything is in order, say 'I do.'"

The tension in the room quadrupled. Both her parents' faces paled. He had said nothing wrong, but the stakes suddenly seemed higher, not knowing if Enrique would follow through with the arrangements made by the two kings—the two fathers—if he found things not in order.

A heavy cloud of uncertainty and stress hung over them.

Madeleine would have to lighten the mood. "Well, if you're planning to say 'I don't,' please speak up before I have the final fitting of my wedding dress. I don't want to spend all that time being a mannequin for nothing."

Enrique tilted his head. "Rest assured, my fair princess, I would never put you through such torture for nothing. I only hope you are as eager to say 'I do' as I am."

Her country would be safe, but she…

Her parents exhaled in unison before her father motioned to the table. "Let's talk over tea."

As soon as everyone was seated, a server filled their gold-rimmed teacups.

Her mother held her cup by the delicate handle, her pinky angled in the perfect position as described in the royal etiquette handbook. "I don't know what life is like on your island, Enrique, but we have afternoon tea every day. A family tradition the king's mother passed down to me when I was a newlywed."

"Madeleine can bring the tradition to La Isla de la Aurora. Nothing can replace Gaullia, but I want your daughter to feel welcome on the island." Enrique spoke without missing a beat. "I will speak with Ortiz, who runs the palace, so he can implement a daily tea service upon our return."

"Thank you." Her mother brightened. "That would be lovely, wouldn't it, Madeleine?"

"Yes, ma'am." At least she could look forward to something every day. She turned to Enrique. "Thank you."

"You're welcome. Our two countries are geographically different, but I hope you'll come to think of the island as home."

"I'm sure she will," her father said before Madeleine could speak. He took the first bite. "Delicious. Help yourself, Enrique."

"Thank you, sir." The crown prince's cucumber sandwich appeared so dainty compared to his large hands before he set it on his plate. He added a scone with a dollop of jelly. "I enjoy afternoon tea. Until my brother's wife, Jules, joined our family, the palace was more of a bachelor pad, which drove our head housekeeper, Elena, crazy. Jules has been a good influence on us."

The king held his teacup midair. "Princess Julianna of Aliestle?"

"Yes, she and my brother, Alejandro, recently celebrated their first wedding anniversary. They don't live at the palace, but they join us for dinner a few times a week. She's a kind-hearted woman and will help Madeleine ease into life on the island."

Okay, so Enrique appeared to be fine with Julianna not being his wife. He sounded almost affectionate toward the woman. Madeleine didn't know if she should be worried or pleased about that. "I look forward to meeting her."

"She'll be at our wedding," he added.

Our wedding rammed into Madeleine's heart like a spear. Bypassing her tea, she reached for a miniature éclair. They were her favorite comfort food so she was grateful the chef included them today.

"You mentioned Princess Julianna." Her mother's brows drew together. "I don't mean to be intrusive…"

"She means nosey," her father added.

"He's correct," her mother said. "We are delighted with how the marriage negotiations have gone. All that remains is for you both to sign the contract and marry. But Julianna was to be your bride. Instead, she married your brother. You speak…fondly of her. Does that mean you accept and approve of their marriage?"

Talk about a loaded question. Madeleine ate her éclair. She was surprised her mother had the courage to ask that question when they needed Enrique more than he needed them. But she was curious, too.

Not because she was worried his heart belonged to another. Hers did, so she wouldn't judge him if that were the case. But she wanted to know what kind of marriage he wanted—a marriage of state, where they had heirs and then lived their own lives, or something else. She hoped he wanted them to live separate except for where their children were concerned because that was her wish. More so now that she'd met him.

She sat taller in her chair. "I would like to know the answer to that question, too."

Chapter Four

Calmly, Enrique wiped his mouth with a linen napkin. He'd expected the question. To be honest, he was surprised no one had asked it during the contract negotiations, but then again his father and King Leon had handled that.

One thing Jules had taught Enrique was how women viewed situations and words differently than men. That was why she'd had him practice how to answer certain questions, including this one. He only hoped he didn't mess up because that was all he'd been doing since he arrived at the castle.

The reason?

Princess Madeleine.

No, he wasn't great in social situations, especially when he felt pressured. Until recently, his father's love had been conditional, so when Enrique had been a boy, he'd turned himself into the king's clone. It was only in the past two years that Enrique was finding his own way, rediscovering whom he wanted to be. Forgetting and moving past the old him, however, wasn't easy to do.

His stress level was high today because of the circumstances, but the real reason for his mistakes was Madeleine herself.

She was…gorgeous.

From head to toe, no matter which way he looked at her, she was beautiful. Her ivory complexion appeared smooth, making his fingers itch to feel its softness. The ice-blue colors of her eyes reminded him of a gemstone—an aquamarine or topaz. He wanted to taste her pink-glossed lips and run his hands through her long brown hair. Her posture, tone, and speech exemplified the traits of a proper princess.

Given the circumstances, she was more than he'd hoped to find in a bride. Not that he'd been expecting a troll, because he'd seen her photograph, but a woman like her had her pick of suitors.

His shoulder muscles tightened. Why choose him when he was at the bottom of the eligible royals list?

Enrique didn't dare ask. Not until they signed the

marriage contract. Maybe not until vows were exchanged. Possibly not even then.

He was counting his blessings because something about the woman resonated with him at a deep level. That had never happened before, and he couldn't wait to explore that as he got to know her better. But first, he needed to answer them.

"I thought you might have questions about my sister-in-law, Jules…Julianna." He spoke in a pleasant, boring tone as if he were discussing a dinner menu, not his ex-fiancée. Jules had warned him to keep his voice steady. Emotion would suggest he was trying to hide his feelings or lying. Neither of which was true. "Ours was an arranged match, negotiated for the benefit of our two countries. No feelings were involved. There was no romantic attachment."

Only the hope they would grow to love each other. A pipe dream, but Gaullia's royal family didn't need to know that.

"During our engagement, I wasn't an attentive fiancé." This he wanted them to understand. "My focus was on work. Not that it mattered, because Julianna fell in love with my brother. Which would have happened whether or not I'd been more present."

The queen's expression grew curiouser. She leaned forward. "Were family dinners uncomfortable?"

Enrique laughed. "When Julianna broke our engagement, she wasn't with Alejandro. The two, however, cared deeply for each other and weren't apart for long. It took us time as a family to work through what happened, but she is perfect for Alejandro and he for her. I harbor no remorse and approve wholeheartedly of their marriage. No one can stand in the way of true love."

Madeleine stared over the lip of her teacup. "That's a romantic sentiment, given you now find yourself in another arranged match."

He appreciated how she spoke her mind. "I've known my duty is to marry for the sake of my country since birth."

Remember, just because you don't love someone at the beginning doesn't mean feelings won't develop. Love can grow over time.

Jules had told him that once. He hoped with all his heart she was correct. Especially now after meeting his intended wife.

"I never expected to find a love match," he admitted. "But Julianna said love can grow over time so I hope that will be the case with us."

There. He'd said it. Now, he wanted to see Madeleine's response.

As her eyes widened, her lips curled. Not into a smile, either. He couldn't tell if she was disgusted or in shock. He hoped the latter.

His gaze met hers. "I don't mean to pressure you, Princess."

She opened her mouth as if to speak, but then she took a sip of her tea.

Was that her way of not answering? Having doubts about their wedding?

About him?

"Princess Julianna is a wise woman," the queen said sincerely. "Love can strike like a lightning bolt or it can build, growing slowly like a white cedar. The latter type lasts longer."

Madeleine placed her teacup on the saucer before taking another éclair.

"Your father mentioned your sister-in-law wouldn't be a problem." King Leon appeared to be younger and in better health than Enrique's father. But a similar wariness was imprinted on the lines of his face and under his tired eyes. "But I appreciate you clarifying the situation for my wife and daughter."

"I'm happy to answer whatever questions you may have, sir." But that didn't mean Enrique would do as well answering them. He raised his teacup. "One unexpected benefit to Alejandro's marriage is our alliance with Aliestle. Once Madeleine and I wed, my father and I will speak with King Alaric about where Gaullia fits into that arrangement."

The relief on the king's face was palpable. Surprising, given most monarchs remained stoic in meetings such as this. Perhaps King Leon saw no obstacles to his daughter's match.

"Aliestle may be a small country, but it holds much power due to their abundance of resources and riches." The king sounded envious. "Given we share a border,

I—our entire country—would be honored and grateful to be included in your alliance."

"We will see that happens, sir. Madeleine's country will be tied to mine." Enrique's gaze flicked from the king to her. "Arranging a formal agreement with your 'neighbor' is not only smart but also strategic."

The statesman in him poured out with a natural confidence. He wished that had happened with his future wife.

"Thank you for understanding." King Leon's smile was more natural. "Gaullia is equally happy to help your island if we can."

"I shall pass that on to my father, but you're already giving up your country's most valuable treasure—your daughter." Enrique was here to meet the entire royal family, but he wanted to focus his attention on Madeleine. Soon, he hoped he would get that chance. "For which, I am grateful."

And he was.

Not only because he would keep the throne after she became his wife, but also because she could prove his heart worked. His attraction to her gave him hope their union would be more than an arrangement for the sake of two countries. He longed to find love. That was his dream—one he'd shared only with Jules—and now it appeared to be on the verge of coming true.

A lightness overtook him. He bit into a berry. Sweetness exploded in his mouth.

Would Madeleine's kiss be as delicious?

The conversation turned to politics, which made Enrique feel more comfortable, but the discussion was surface-level and cautious, as if each participant was feeling out the other's beliefs and trigger points. At least that was how he felt.

"The future lies with our youth," Enrique said without too much worry. "Education must be a priority or the next generations will be ill-equipped to move into the job sector and public service."

The queen beamed. "Did you know Madeleine has a strong interest in education reform?"

The king's eyes brightened. "You'll be able to work together on your initiatives."

"Yes." As Enrique leaned toward her, a citrusy floral fragrance tickled his nose. He didn't know if the scent was her perfume or shampoo, but he liked it. "I look forward to hearing your thoughts."

Madeleine's smile appeared forced. She must still be nervous. "And I yours."

She reached for another éclair.

Definitely nervous given her need for sugar.

Maybe he could lighten the mood and put her at ease.

He motioned to the chocolate-covered pastry in her hand. "I see you enjoy sweets."

She nodded. "The chef made these as a special treat for your visit. They're my favorite."

Enrique smiled. "Perhaps later, you can show me around the grounds and point out your favorite spots."

"A walk would be nice," she said.

Enrique picked up a slice of crostini covered with *foie gras mousse* and a dab of jam. "Walking is an excellent way to burn calories, too, since you are splurging on more éclairs."

Her lips parted.

He waited for her smile, only it didn't come.

Madeleine placed the éclair on her plate before raising her teacup.

Oh, no. Enrique's heart dropped. Her reaction was not what he'd expected after making a joke. He hadn't mentioned body parts so he wasn't sure why they hadn't laughed. Her parents' grim faces told him they misinterpreted what they heard.

Should he try to repair the damage now or wait?

Madeleine's tight body language told him it didn't matter—she wouldn't forgive him either way.

He couldn't blame her.

As the day butler escorted Enrique out of the sitting room, Madeleine kept her hands clasped on her lap, and her lips pressed together. A way she'd been sitting for the past thirty minutes. All she wanted was for Enrique to go away.

He glanced over his shoulder at her.

She met his gaze for a nanosecond before staring

at the ornate rug beneath her shoes. Otherwise, she might not be polite.

The sound of footsteps decreased until they disappeared.

Madeleine had never cherished silence more.

The crown prince was being taken to his suite, but she wished he was leaving the palace—the country—instead.

"Please, Father. He's…" She kept her voice calm and steady, but listing the adjectives to describe Enrique would upset her. "Isn't there anyone else I can marry?"

A vein pulsed at his jaw. "No."

"Aliestle has four princes." Desperation laced her words. Nothing in her years of princess training or experience had prepared her for…him. She had no idea how she'd survived the tea without bolting. Oh, she'd been tempted to after his calorie comment. "Perhaps one of them—"

"Crown Prince Brandt is closest to you in age, but he's still younger and was betrothed as a child. The other three princes are much too young." Her father's gaze softened. "Give Enrique time. He's smitten with you. That much is clear."

Smitten? *Ugh.* That was the last thing she wanted.

Madeleine ate the rest of her éclair. Maybe if she kept eating them, she would no longer fit into her gown so there wouldn't be a wedding.

"And he's romantic," her mother added with a lilt

to her voice. "That should bode well."

Anger flared, but Madeleine kept it under check. "I'm not looking for a love match. My heart is spoken for."

Her mother reached for her. "It's been five years. Louie wouldn't want you to close yourself off. He would want you to fall in love again and live for the both of you."

Madeleine shook her head, too forcefully because the room tilted. "I…can't."

Not that she'd tried. Oh, she'd gone out on a handful of dates, ones forced upon her by well-meaning family. But all had been uncomfortable. Any kisses, however brief, had made her feel sick. But today…

It had been a disaster. To imagine a lifetime of feeling like this…

She clutched her stomach.

Her father shook his head. "The meeting didn't go that badly."

Madeleine stared in disbelief. "He suggested I'd get fat eating éclairs. Not to mention slighting Gaullia. And—"

"Nerves," her mother interrupted in a stern voice. "You should have seen your father before our wedding. Each time he opened his mouth, something wrong came out. My parents were mortified, but my country needed the match so I was…stuck."

"With time and patience," her father said. "I came

around."

Her mother nodded. "And so will Enrique. He needs to adjust and mature."

"He's not a teenager. He's over thirty. Thirty-five to be exact." Madeleine's mind was made up. "He's…dreadful."

"You're being a drama princess which doesn't suit you." Her father's tone turned kingly. "Enrique appears eager to marry you."

"Because no one else wants him for a husband," she muttered.

"Madeleine-Victoria." Her mother's harsh voice echoed in the room. "That is not how a proper princess talks about her future spouse—or anyone. Enrique is your only choice. We've been over the reasons, and you agreed. Now, behave yourself before we find ourselves without a country to call home. I wouldn't put it past that tyrant Alaric to take all the land."

Duly chastised, Madeleine bowed her head. "Excuse my outburst, sir and ma'am. I don't wish to cause harm to Gaullia. I know my duty, and I won't let you down."

"Let Enrique get settled and then take him on a tour of the grounds," her father ordered.

"And if there's a chance to kiss him during your walk, do." Her mother patted Madeleine's hand. "That might seal the deal."

Madeleine's stomach churned. She didn't want to touch Enrique. Forget about kissing him.

But he was to be her husband—the father of her children.

Which meant she'd be doing more than kissing him once they wed. She wrapped her hands around her stomach.

For the first time in her life, she wished she hadn't been born a princess.

Chapter Five

Phone pressed against his ear, Enrique paced the length of his suite. His shoes sank into the plush carpet.

The room was a pleasant blue, but he only saw red because of his stupidity. He'd made a fool of himself earlier. More than once. Which was the last thing he and his family had wanted to happen. "I'm making a mess of everything."

"A literal mess?" Jules asked, her voice calm.

She'd been so perfect—the definition of what a princess and future queen should be, but two years of racing sailboats, battling the weather, the waves, and sometimes discrimination, had given her an even stronger steadiness he envied.

"I didn't spill anything, but my words came out…wrong." Twenty other adjectives would work, but he might feel worse and worry Jules. He hated burdening her, but she was the only one who knew what he'd overheard his mother saying about him years ago and the effect the words had on him.

"During the tea?" Jules asked.

"Yes." He wished that had been his only mistake. "And as soon as I arrived, too. I knew what I wanted to say, but the words weren't as clear as I hoped they'd be. Who am I kidding? I came across as a pompous, self-righteous jerk."

Which was exactly how most royals perceived him.

He had been. But he was trying to change. Emphasis on *trying*. More often than not, his awkwardness and nerves got the best of him in social situations.

"What did you say?" Jules asked.

Enrique quickened his steps. "The first time?"

"Let's start there." Worry edged her words. She was likely biting off her lipstick from her lower lip.

"During the flight, I read a report on Gaullia's windmills and farms. That must have stayed on my mind because when I spoke about their country I sounded less than complimentary about what they have to offer."

"That's not so bad. Claim ignorance. Or tiredness from travel. White lies, but both aren't too big of stretches."

"Lying to the woman I need to marry isn't the way I want to start off our relationship."

"Excellent answer," Jules replied without missing a beat. "So be as honest with her as you are being with me."

"You're easy to talk to, but Madeleine..." He grimaced. "I forgot how to compliment her. Alejandro had said that was important and helped me practice. But instead of saying one thing, I said all three. It was...awkward."

"You're being too hard on yourself. She may have found your mishaps adorable."

He recalled Madeleine's expression and cringed. "She didn't. I don't know why I turn into a twelve-year-old in situations like this. Though most children would be more eloquent than me."

"Nerves," Jules offered in the same big-sister tone she used when she spoke to her four younger brothers. "When a person gets nervous, words fly from their mouth."

"Words were flying, unfortunately."

Silence filled the line. "What else did you say?"

His face heated. If he could take back anything...

"Enrique?" she pressed.

"I suggested walking would be a good way to burn calories with all the éclairs Madeleine was eating."

A groan sounded on the other end of the line. "Remember what happened the last time you did this. You *never* mention a woman's weight or any body parts, especially in conjunction with dessert. Not ever. Even as a compliment because you don't know what's happening in her life or with her health. We went over this."

He hung his head but didn't stop pacing across the room again. "I know, but I never expected… Madeleine is…"

"What?"

Enrique sighed. He couldn't help himself. "Beautiful. No, stunning."

"You like her."

"I don't know her, but…" He pictured Madeleine's ice-blue eyes, high cheekbones, and full lips. His pulse kicked up a notch. "She could have any man. I don't know why she's marrying me."

"She's matched to you. You'll be king."

"We haven't signed the contract yet. And even then, that's no guarantee—"

"The wedding plans are underway."

"Yes, but given my performance so far, she might call off the wedding."

"Stop performing and act more naturally. You can't pretend to be something you're not. You need to step up. Apologize for what you said. Grovel, if you must."

He recalled the glances passing among the royal

family members. He'd offended them as much as Madeleine. "I will."

"Think before you speak. You don't want to make a fool of yourself."

"Too late, but I hope not to repeat that."

"You know what's at stake."

"I do." Which was why he had to do his best and make no additional mistakes. In the past two years, he'd been turning around his country's economy and revamping the education system. This was one more task to accomplish. "I will be more careful."

"Don't get down on yourself." Jules's voice was soft but full of strength. "You know what happens then."

"I won't drown my sorrows in alcohol again." He'd done that twice. Once after Jules had broken off their engagement. The second time was when another princess—one he'd hoped to marry after the new succession law had gone into effect—had told him she wasn't interested in a match after stringing him along for weeks. Okay, four weeks. But that had been the longest any woman besides Jules had put up with him so he'd been…hopeful. "The odds, however—"

"You have no idea the impression you made on the princess."

Yes, he did. Which was why he would likely wear a path in the carpet. "Madeleine doesn't like me."

"You don't—"

"It's true. I might not be an expert on the opposite

sex like my brother, but she barely tolerated me. And I don't blame her. I was more ogre than prince." Enrique blew out a breath. "Start preparing Alejandro."

"No." The word rushed out. "You just arrived in Gaullia."

"And as soon as I exited the limo and opened my mouth, I screwed up." A pain seared Enrique's chest. "You think I'm being dramatic, but I can't have my brother blindsided. He agreed to my plan, but I don't believe he thought I would fail. It's a ninety percent chance he will be the next king."

"Ninety?" Disbelief filled her voice.

Ninety-nine, but Enrique didn't want to upset Jules. "Yes."

A beat passed. And another.

"I will speak with Alejandro." The sharpness of her words suggested she was fighting her own battle of emotions. "But please, promise me, you won't give up hope."

Hope was all Enrique had left. He didn't know how much remained after the tea. A glimmer, perhaps. Even though Jules couldn't see him, he forced a smile. Maybe that would keep him from sounding so…dejected. "I won't."

"I'm sorry."

The compassion in those two words slayed him. The knot in his stomach doubled. "It's not your fault."

"If Alejandro and I had waited to marry—"

"Parliament would have done something else to

the succession laws." Enrique hated interrupting, but he needed Jules to understand. Maybe then she wouldn't sound so distraught. "Father believes they want to end the monarchy. Alejandro must see that doesn't happen."

"You're giving up. I can tell by your tone. Please don't. Keep trying. No matter what. The island needs you." Her words poured out, fast and full of emotion.

Enrique hated that. He wanted her, his brother, and his father to be proud of him, but he feared he would disappoint them all. Still, he had brought them to this point. The blame was his and his alone.

"I'm not giving up," he said loudly. Realizing where he was and not knowing if the rooms were soundproof, he lowered his voice. "I'm being...realistic."

"I don't like your realism."

That made him laugh. Some tension seeped away. "You're right about the island. It and the people need us more than Parliament realizes. That is my biggest concern."

More so than what happened to him.

"Alejandro will make sure nothing changes." Her confidence brimmed across the miles. "And so will I."

Enrique exhaled. He hoped his stress would disappear as easily as his breath. "Thank you. Again."

A knock sounded at the door.

"I must go. I'll talk to you soon."

As he disconnected from the call, he went to the

door and opened it. Madeleine stood there with a tentative closed-mouth smile. Another forced one.

"Hello." He hadn't thought before speaking but a greeting shouldn't affect her opinion of him negatively. At least he hoped not. "What a pleasant surprise. I wasn't expecting to see you so soon."

She stood with her shoulders pressed back and head held high. Proper princess posture. "You mentioned touring the grounds earlier."

"I did, but first, I must apologize." Enrique forced the words from his dry throat before realizing he was still putting on an act of what he thought she wanted him to be. He took another breath, allowing his posture to relax. "I'm sorry for offending you earlier. I wish I could blame what I said on nerves, but that wasn't the case. I'm known for saying the wrong things. Not just at the wrong time. Pretty much all the time. I've been trying to do better, but I still have a ways to go as you saw today."

A beat passed. Then another.

He forced himself not to shift his weight between his feet. She was the offended party, not him.

Madeleine raised her chin slightly. "Apology accepted."

Enrique waited for her to say more, but she didn't. "May we begin again?"

She nodded.

He extended his arm. "I'm Enrique. Crown prince or court jester depending on the situation."

A smile tugged at the corners of her lips. She shook his hand. "I'm Madeleine. Proper princess and tour guide extraordinaire."

His hand was larger, but her grip was stronger than he imagined it would be. Her skin was as soft and smooth as it looked.

She drew her arm to her side, and he missed her warmth.

He stepped out of his room and closed the door behind him. "Lead the way, tour guide."

As Madeleine headed down the wide hallway, she motioned to various doors they passed. "This is the family wing. There are four guest suites besides my family's rooms."

"Do you host many guests?"

"Around the holidays, mainly. There's also a summer celebration that is popular. Most guests stay on the other side of the castle, though."

"I'm honored to be near you."

Her expression didn't change, but she no longer frowned. That was progress.

She opened a door to a landing and stone staircase. "This will take us to the ground level."

On either side of the steps were walls of rocks put together like puzzle pieces and held in place by mortar. The castle oozed character, as if part of a movie set.

"Is this original?" he asked.

"Yes." She didn't slow her pace. "The exterior looks the same as it has for centuries albeit maintained by the staff and updated as necessary."

He ran his hand along the rocks to his right. The stone was worn smooth. "If these walls could talk."

She glanced over her shoulder with a surprised gaze. "They might have stories to tell. This was the escape route for the royal family when the castle was attacked. That happened a few times with past generations."

"When we are on the island, I'll show you what my family used."

"I—I'd like that."

Her voice was hesitant, but that was better than disgusted. More progress.

The staircase led to a small grassy area enclosed by another wall—this one taller. He followed her to a massive iron gate. "Is this to keep the royal family in or others out?"

"I daresay both." She sounded as if she were smiling. "When we were children, Karl was known for getting into mischief."

"What about you?"

She shrugged. "Someone had to behave."

That sounded like Jules. Did Madeleine have a secret passion as his sister-in-law had? He would ask once they were getting along better.

He followed her out of the gate to a landscaped area with clipped hedges, stone walkways, and verdant shrubbery. "This is breathtaking."

She glanced around as if seeing the grounds for the

first time. "It is. I take the beauty for granted or remember when snow covers everything during the winter."

"The weather is harsher than on the island."

Madeleine nodded. "I've lived here for twenty-seven years so I'm used to it. Sunshine and blue skies overhead for most of the year will be different."

Her words held no anticipation. No excitement. No happiness.

Yes, this was an arranged marriage, but her lack of emotion bothered him. "Will you miss Gaullia?"

"I've always known this place wouldn't be my home forever."

She hadn't answered the question. Not exactly. But he wouldn't push. Not until he knew where he stood with her.

"Would you like to see the garden?" she asked.

"Yes, please."

As they approached rose bushes with bursts of colorful blooms, a large fountain caught his attention. No water flowed. "Is the fountain broken?"

She inhaled sharply. "It—"

"You're trembling." He touched her arm. "Please, let's sit."

He led her to a nearby bench.

She took a breath and exhaled slowly. "I'm sorry."

Enrique noticed the quiver of her lower lip. Something was wrong. "Should I get your mother or maid?"

Madeleine shook her head. "I don't come out here that often, and when I do, I…"

"Does the fountain have special meaning to you?" he asked.

She nodded. "I should tell you so you don't hear it from anyone else."

"There's no rush."

"Given we marry in ten days, I'd say there is." She reached for her throat before clasping her hands together. "Were you told about my previous fiancé?"

It was his turn to nod. "Louie was a few years behind me at boarding school. He was a great guy. I'm sorry for your loss."

"He was. A great guy, I mean. The best." She took a quick breath. "He died days before our wedding."

Enrique remembered. Much of Europe had mourned the crown prince's death. "Helicopter crash."

"Yes." Eyes gleaming, she stared at the fountain. "The fountain was a gift from him to my family to celebrate our wedding. My father turned it on after the funeral. It worked perfectly, shooting water thirty feet in the air, before cascading through the bowls and into the larger pool. I slept out here that night, but the next day it broke." She half laughed. "Karl told me it was Louie's way of telling me to sleep in my bed."

"That could be one interpretation."

"But not mine," she admitted. "My father had the fountain repaired, but it kept breaking. Finally, after a month of this, I told him not to bother fixing it again."

Her rough breaths. The crack in her voice. Her sad eyes.

All signs of her grief.

He envied Louie for eliciting such a response in Madeleine. "You loved him."

"Very much." She spoke softly, but her saying those two words brought a light to her eyes. Something that had been missing before. "Ours wasn't an arranged match. We went to our parents and asked to wed. Both his and mine agreed though they made us wait until I finished college."

That was news to Enrique. "You were fortunate."

"We were." She bit her lip. "I was supposed to be on the helicopter with Louie, but my mother wanted one final fitting for my wedding gown. Demanded it. So I stayed here, and he…"

Her sorrowful expression brought a pain to Enrique's chest. "You still love Louie."

"I do." She didn't hesitate answering. "Do you believe in true love?"

He nearly laughed. Two years ago, love had seemed like something that only happened in the movies. "I didn't until seeing my brother and Jules together. Now, I do."

"Louie was mine."

The words resonated through Enrique. Something in his heart shifted. Something unexpected and unfamiliar that hurt.

"I thought you should know," Madeleine added.

"After Louie's death, I knew an arranged marriage awaited me. I also know heirs are expected, but I'm not looking for…"

"A love match." Enrique forced the words from his tight throat.

"I hope you understand. It's not you."

Disappointment grabbed hold of him because he'd wanted to fall in love. He'd wanted to prove his mother wrong. For the best, he realized. Whether or not Madeleine's heart was taken, a woman like her would never love him. At least by marrying her, he would keep the throne and provide heirs. That would deem their match a success. She could continue to love Louie, too.

Enrique ignored the ache inside him. This wasn't the marriage he envisioned for himself, but any union would be better than losing the throne. Even a loveless one. "I understand."

She straightened. "Can you accept that my heart belongs to another and always will?"

Again, her speaking so plainly about this hurt, but that had to do with his ego. Nothing else. "Yes, because I never expected to marry for love."

That much was true. Even if he'd been hoping for more since Jules told him he was capable of loving. But dreams didn't always come true. He'd survived without love this long. He could continue to live that way.

"An arranged marriage to benefit my country and my bride's has always been viewed as the best option." *The only option now.* "My parents didn't love each other.

They divorced when I was a child. That hurt me and my brother and distorted our views of relationships. I don't want that for my children. I hope we can co-parent with respect for one another."

Silence.

No doubt, she had learned the lesson of thinking before speaking. Each passing second, however, increased the tension in the air.

"I want that for our children, too," she said finally.

He blew out a breath. "Excellent."

The lines didn't disappear from her forehead, but they lessened. "Would you like to see our garden now?"

"I would." He stood. "Gardening is my hobby."

She rose. "Then you may be disappointed. Ours have much room for improvement."

"Gardens must be tended to grow properly." He noticed a few bushes that needed pruning, but he wasn't about to open his mouth and insert his foot again. "A little extra care and patience does wonders."

She smiled. Still closed-mouth, but the action appeared less forced this time. "You should speak to our lawn and garden staff. I'm sure they would appreciate your input."

"I would be happy to." Enrique bowed before extending his arm to her. "Shall we see how much work needs to be done?"

Chapter Six

Walking through the garden with Enrique, Madeleine realized she'd underestimated him. Yes, he'd been horrendous when he arrived, but he'd apologized. Since then, only one thing he'd said could be misconstrued. Because she was hypersensitive to him, she'd given the crown prince the benefit of the doubt.

Shade from a large tree provided relief from the hot sun. As they passed under the branches, birds flew away, rustling the leaves.

Enrique went to the tree trunk and outlined the

three sets of initials carved in the trunk. "Even proper princesses get into mischief."

"Karl and Louie talked me into it." The way her words rushed out sent heat rushing up her neck. "I told them it would be a bad idea, but they wouldn't listen."

"That's what they all say," Enrique teased.

"It's true." Madeleine laughed. "Though I see now why no adult believed me since my initials are there, too. Louie tried to convince Mrs. Hobbs I was an innocent bystander, but she didn't believe him."

Enrique studied the initials before glancing at Madeleine. "You knew Louie for a long time."

It wasn't a question, but still she answered. "My entire life. Our parents were…are close. He was Karl's best friend for as long as I remember, and then Louie became mine."

"Did Mrs. Hobbs punish you?"

"Yes. She scolded us. Karl was used to that, but it was the first time for me. I was mortified because I rarely got into trouble," Madeleine admitted. "Then she had us report to the master gardener for weeding duty. Karl complained the entire time."

"Was it that horrible?"

Thinking back, she couldn't help but smile. Louie hadn't left her side. "No, I had fun."

"Gardening is fun. Even weeding because you can see the fruits of your efforts right away." Enrique's grin lit up his handsome face. "If being handed over to the master gardener would have been my punishment, I would have gotten into lots of trouble."

"How were you punished?"

"I wasn't." He focused on the tree again. "I did what I was told. Emulated my father to a ridiculous degree. My brother was the troublemaker in the family."

Something in his voice piqued her curiosity. "Are the two of you close?"

"We were, and then we weren't." Enrique ran his fingertip through the "L." "Things are better now."

She had a feeling there was more of a story there. Maybe one day, he would share that.

"Alejandro lived to sail—he still does—but I wanted to dig in the dirt. It annoyed our father so I woke up early and worked with our gardener then."

The wistfulness in his voice intrigued her. "Do you do that now?"

He half laughed. "Not as I used to, because of my responsibilities. But I do whenever I can and have a weekly meeting with our landscaping staff."

That explained the roughness of his hands. "Your garden must be beautiful."

"The flowers I sent you came from it. I cut the stems myself."

His thoughtfulness touched her heart. "They are lovely. Thank you."

He faced her. "Thank you for bringing me out here. I could spend hours looking at everything."

"Digging and pruning, too?"

"Of course."

An image of the crown prince dressed casually with sweat glistening his skin and his muscles straining filled her head. She swallowed. "I'll let the master gardener know he may have company while you're here."

Her voice sounded husky. That was…odd. She cleared her throat.

Enrique went to a nearby rose bush. He bent to study a pink-orange blossom. "What a lovely shade."

"That's my mother's favorite. It's called the Victory Anne after her."

Straightening, he glanced at Madeleine. "Based on what I saw during tea, the name fits."

"She likes you."

"That could change." Amusement danced in his eyes. "Which flower is your favorite?"

She thought for a moment before shrugging. "I don't have one. Chocolate is the way to my heart."

His brows drew together. "Chocolate and white fabric are a dangerous combination. We must find you a favorite flower before the wedding so one is in your bouquet."

"It might not match what's been planned."

He rubbed his chin. "Then we hide it under a blossom that coordinates. Every bride should carry at least one of her favorite flowers."

"Says who?"

"Me." He examined pink blossoms on another bush. "This may be an arranged marriage, but that doesn't mean the wedding can't be special. Our children might ask questions about it someday."

This Enrique didn't seem to be the same man who'd arrived and had tea with her. The version with her now seemed as romantic as the earlier one talking about how love could grow.

At least he knew that wasn't a possibility now. Enrique's understanding and acceptance of that likely explained why his mentioning the bouquet and their children hadn't sent her into full meltdown mode. But she'd rather not talk about their wedding or…future. That would happen soon enough.

"What is your favorite flower?" she asked.

"It depends on the day and my mood. Each is beautiful and unique with its own appeal. Which is why your bouquet was a mix."

Interesting, but that begged a question. "Yet you ask me to choose a favorite?"

He motioned to the nearest rose bush, but his gaze remained on her. "Many see a flower that captures their attention. Something about the shape or the color or the scent or an event associated with it. For whatever reason, it becomes the one. Their favorite. To bring comfort or a smile or maybe just a memory."

Enrique was an enigma. He lacked a conversation filter, but he'd showed surprising compassion and sensitivity during their earlier discussion about Louie. Examining the rows of plants brought out a lightness in Enrique, showing her a softer, kinder side.

One she liked. "Daisy."

"Daisy?" he repeated.

"That's my favorite flower."

"A surprising choice for a princess."

Madeleine shrugged, but she had her reason for picking that kind.

"Louie gave you daisies."

Again, it wasn't a question, but she nodded.

"Does the memory make you happy?" Enrique asked.

As she thought about those daisies from so long ago, warmth spread through her. "Yes."

"Then we'll have the florist add them."

His voice held no uncertainty, reminding Madeleine of her father. What the king commanded happened, whether or not people agreed. She had a feeling a daisy would be in her bridal bouquet. More than one.

"Thank you." She'd known wearing Louie's ring on her wedding day wouldn't be appropriate, but a reminder of him would be with her. "I appreciate your thoughtfulness."

"Ignoring what happened before we met would be wrong. Our pasts are part of who we are. Love may not grow between us, but I hope respect and friendship will."

What he said both shocked and pleased her. "So do I."

"I also suggest future important discussions should

happen in a garden," he joked. "I seem to say the right words more easily out here."

"Or you are becoming more comfortable in Gaullia."

"And around you." His words touched Madeleine like a caress—soft and warm and meant only for her—providing a connection she hadn't felt with anyone in years.

They stared at each other.

"Mads!" Karl yelled, breaking the silence.

She glanced in the direction of her brother's voice and waved her arm. "Over here."

He strode toward her. "Father wants you both in his office. It's time to review and sign the marriage agreement."

Her hand flew to cover the ring she wore beneath her shirt. That always brought her comfort no matter the situation or how powerless she felt.

"Is something wrong, Madeleine?" The concern in Enrique's eyes matched his expression. His arm hovered between them as if he couldn't decide whether or not to reach out to her. "Would you rather wait to sign the agreement?"

"No!" she and Karl shouted at the same time.

Madeleine shot a glance at her brother. "The signing is a formality my parents won't put off given the efforts going into the wedding planning. I can show you more of the garden tomorrow."

Enrique's gaze bounced between her and her

brother. The lines on his forehead deepened. "Okay."

Tension replaced the comfortable atmosphere from moments ago. "Let's go."

The three walked to the castle in silence. Each step sent wild thoughts swirling in her mind. What if she refused to sign the document? Not that she would, but the thought opened up a hundred different possibilities. Some ordinary, others far-fetched.

What if she ran away and became a trapeze performer in a circus? No, clowns terrified her. She would never survive working with them.

What if she became a social media influencer? Though if she were stripped of her title that might not work. Besides, she wasn't sure anyone would care what she wore or the makeup she used or where she vacationed.

What if she did what most people did—move away from home and get a job? Being a royal had to provide her with a marketable skill. She had a master's degree, too, though she hadn't used it much. She hadn't lived on her own except during college. Even then, she hadn't paid her own bills.

Karl held open a door for her. "After you."

Not that she would do anything except marry as her parents requested. That was her duty—her fate.

Madeleine went through the music room. Enrique followed her.

She passed her father's loyal assistant and the two royal guards flanking each side of the door to the king's inner sanctum—the same way she had hours earlier. She acknowledged each with a nod before entering the office.

Her father and mother stood behind the desk. Their attorney, Mr. Sanderson, stood on the opposite side.

"Come in, come in." Her father motioned them inside. "Everything is ready for you to sign."

Those were the same words her father had said when she and Louie signed their agreement. Even though they'd been a love match, a marriage contract had been drawn up. That was the custom when royal families merged.

This time, however, the entire wedding wasn't about two people in love. This was about forging an alliance between two countries. Three, if she wanted to be exact.

As she moved toward the desk, Madeleine's heart pounded against her rib cage. Each beat was a countdown to the end of her life in Gaullia with her family and a new one on La Isla de la Aurora with Enrique. "We're ready."

"Yes, sir." Enrique sounded upbeat. "We are."

Her father's smile spread ear to ear. "Then, let's not waste any time. I have reviewed the marriage contract. King Dario is going over his copy as we speak. Sit so we can get started."

They did. Karl stood behind them.

"Your Highnesses." Mr. Sanderson handed them

each a document. "These are copies for you to read. You'll sign the original contract."

She'd known this was coming, but seeing her name listed with Enrique's surprised her. The black letters against the stark white paper was the final death knell to her wish to avoid marriage.

Even though she'd complained and made excuses about having to marry Enrique, it wasn't him, *per se*. If she were being honest with herself, she didn't want another match to a royal. The truth was she didn't want to marry anyone.

Enrique turned the top page. "I've always believed reading the fine print was important."

She opened her copy. "Too many people skip that part."

He glanced her way. "Not you."

"Not me." She remembered something she'd seen on the internet. "Wouldn't want to sell my soul to a computer game company by accident."

"Or give away our oldest child for Wi-Fi access."

Madeleine smiled at his conspiratorial tone. She'd read about that one, too. At least they shared something in common besides being royalty.

Love may not grow between us, but I hope respect and friendship will.

She wanted that, too.

As she stared at the page, the words blurred. She blinked and then refocused.

The contract contained the typical legalese. The

document could have been written without the multi-syllable words, but then what would the attorneys do with their time?

She reached the part about her dowry—heirloom jewelry, a large estate near the border, and money coming from a trust she'd inherited after her maternal grandparents' deaths. The property had been a new addition to keep King Alaric from stealing the land that now belonged to his in-laws. That sounded more like something her mother would have thought of than her father.

"I have a question, Mr. Sanderson," Enrique said to the attorney. "Clause ten point three regarding heirs."

The lawyer turned to that page. So did Madeleine since she hadn't read that far yet.

"It talks about the dissolution of the royal marriage if an heir isn't conceived within five years," Enrique said, glancing at the document in his hands. "I've never heard of that clause in a marriage contract."

"It is part of all Gaullia marriage agreements and has been for two, possibly three, generations," Mr. Sanderson explained. "Heirs are required for a monarchy to survive so this clause is in place for a ruler's protection."

It had been in her contract with Louie. She hadn't thought twice about it. Neither had he.

"Did my father know about this ahead of time?" Enrique asked.

"Yes," King Leon answered. "He agreed to the clause. As Mr. Sanderson explained, this ensures the line of succession. Nothing more."

Enrique turned the page. "What follows is basically a prenuptial agreement and how a divorce would be handled."

Mr. Sanderson smiled. "That is only to protect the assets of both parties, and countries, should the marriage end."

"My parents are divorced so I know how difficult the end of a marriage can be, but this reads more like an escape clause." Enrique angled his shoulders toward her. "Are you okay with this, my princess?"

She glanced at her father who nodded slightly. "Yes. This was in my first contract, too. I'm fine with it."

For a royal marriage to be successful, heirs were required. This clause saw to that. Sure, the timeframe might push up when a couple started a family, but she prayed it didn't take her five years to get pregnant. The sooner children were born meant she could focus on being a mother rather than being a wife.

"That was my only question. If Madeleine is fine with the clause, so am I." Enrique placed the front page on top. "Everything else is as my father said. I'm ready to sign."

A collective breath appeared to be released by each member of her family.

Now, it was her turn. "I'm ready to sign as well."

Mr. Sanderson removed the original document from a leather pouch and opened to the last page. He handed Enrique a fancy pen. "You will sign first, sir."

Enrique gave her an encouraging smile before placing a bold signature on the page. He handed her the pen. "Your turn."

Don't think.

Just sign.

The pen made no sound against the paper, but she heard the latch of a lock on her heart.

It was done.

Her country would soon be safe. All that remained was the wedding ceremony. She placed the pen on the desk.

Mr. Sanderson put the original contract in the leather pouch. He gathered the printouts. "Thank you, Your Highnesses. Copies of the signed agreement will be delivered shortly. Congratulations on your engagement."

Enrique shook the man's hand. "Thank you."

"We appreciate your assistance with this." She couldn't muster much enthusiasm. If Mr. Sanderson and the other of the country's legal council had been smarter about the loan terms, a royal wedding wouldn't be taking place. "Is there anything else you need from us?"

The attorney patted the pouch. "I have all I need."

She stood. "Then I'll excuse myself."

Enrique rose. "Thank you."

She made a beeline for the parlor, what her mother called the smaller of two libraries in the castle.

He followed Madeleine.

She sat at her embroidery stand and pulled out a needle.

Enrique entered the room. Coming closer, he peered down at her piece. "You made the embroidery artwork hanging on the walls."

"I did." She brought the needle through the bottom of the canvas. "You enjoy gardening. This is my escape. A governess loved Jane Austen. She believed a princess, even a modern-day one, needed certain skills. I can't balance a checkbook, but I know how to create magic with a needle and thread."

"I'm sorry."

She glanced up at him. "For?"

"Us having to get married."

Her chest tightened. "It is inevitable. If not to you then someone else. I didn't mean to be rude leaving my father's office without saying a word. I needed…"

"…Space."

"And time," she admitted. "It's not you."

His expression suggested he didn't believe her.

"Okay, you're part of it," she admitted. "But I wasn't ready to jump into wedding talk as soon as we signed the contract."

"So you came here instead."

"I enjoy it as you do with your garden."

He inspected her work closer. "You're talented."

"I've had years of practice."

"Teach me."

His words startled her. "You want to learn embroidery?"

"Yes."

She stiffened. Karl and Louie used to make fun of her, calling her embroidery a waste of time when she could do something else like being with them and playing video games. Her father barely paid attention to the items she'd made. "Why?"

"Gardening is my passion. This is yours." Enrique held up his hands. "I'm sure I'll be all thumbs, but I would like to try."

The man kept surprising her, only now in good ways. She patted the spot next to her on the sofa.

He sat.

She reached down to the basket of supplies to grab a needle and a skein of thread. "The first thing you need to do is thread the needle."

Enrique laughed. "Starting at the beginning."

"That's how you learn to do it the proper way."

He rubbed his palms on his pant legs and then took the items from her.

The needle and thread looked tiny compared to his hands. "Ready?"

"No, but that hasn't stopped me yet."

She laughed. Nothing could stop a signed marriage contract, but for now, she would forget about that. About everything. And enjoy herself.

Chapter Seven

One day of public appearances with Madeleine and the royal family turned into another. Enrique understood the obligations leading up to the wedding. Part of the preparations meant being seen together and interviewed, especially since people knew they'd only just met. Opinion was split on the short engagement. Unfortunately, Enrique hadn't helped matters.

Leaving his room, he closed the door and went to Madeleine's. Tonight, Karl was throwing them a small engagement party. Small meaning less than two hundred people were expected at the black-tie event.

Things weren't going as smoothly as he'd hoped. He'd made two *faux pas* in the last twenty-four hours. One in private that only Karl and Madeleine witnessed, but the other was in public with the press nearby.

Enrique cringed. That led to him telling Madeleine about his fear of germs and getting sick because he'd been hospitalized as a child and left there for days with only a royal guard outside his door and no one to keep him company. An excuse, yes, but one that explained his disastrous visit to the children's hospital.

He'd issued an apology for asking to wear a hazmat suit and sent gifts to each patient without being told it was necessary, but that didn't fix the damage he'd done.

Madeleine wasn't happy, but she hadn't been angry with him. She stood by his side as he apologized, and then she relayed the story of him being alone in the hospital as a child so people would understand what motivated his actions.

He'd appreciated her support, and that she hadn't asked to be released from the marriage contract.

Yet something felt…

Not *off.*

Missing.

Unlike Alejandro and Julianna, whose relationship had been deemed a modern day fairy tale by the press and the public, no one expected Enrique and Madeleine to act like a couple in love. No hand-holding or tender glances or other displays of affection were required. Their upcoming marriage was being viewed as a business transaction.

Which it was.

And would remain one long after saying "I do."

No matter how many children they had.

But he wished for more. For...

Love.

A happily ever after.

What his brother had found.

Enrique wasn't vain enough to think he would have had that with Jules if they had married, but he'd hoped to find that someday. Now...

He stood in front of Madeleine's bedroom door.

Get over it.

That kind of relationship was nothing more than a fantasy, one he hadn't indulged himself with even as a child. No need to do so now.

He had no reason to complain given what he would receive by marrying Madeleine—the crown. Ruling the island mattered the most. Enrique needed to focus on the end goal. Being king was why he was getting married.

Not to find love.

Not everyone was as lucky as his brother and sister-in-law. Some people never fell in love. His parents hadn't. Other royals barely tolerated their spouses despite decades of marriage.

He didn't want that.

Which was why he wanted to get along with Madeleine.

Romantic love wasn't a possibility, but friendship was. That would provide enough of a basis for their marriage and allow their children to thrive and not worry whether an argument might spell the end of their mother and father living together.

Enrique straightened his cummerbund before knocking on the door.

Madeleine opened it. She wore a stunning blue evening gown. Her hair was piled on her head in a stylish updo with curly tendrils framing her lovely face. Diamonds sparkled from her earlobes and around her neck.

He realized he was gawking. "You are beautiful, my princess."

She curtsied. "Nice tux."

His chest puffed out. "Thank you."

"We have a few minutes until we're expected downstairs."

"Good, because there's something I wanted to say." He ignored the urge to loosen his bow tie. "May I come in?"

"Yes, but I'll leave my door open since there's no chaperone."

"We don't want to scandalize anyone." Especially her parents. "It is only the twenty-first century."

She laughed. "Someday, these silly rules will no longer matter."

"I hope it's sooner rather than later, but I promise, your virtue is safe with me."

He entered the room. A queen-sized bed was against a wall of windows. A loveseat, chair, and coffee table were in front of a fireplace. The blush pink and gold color scheme was elegant, understated, and feminine, much like Madeleine herself.

The bouquet he'd sent sat on her nightstand. Stems were missing, but he hadn't expected the flowers to last that long. The only photograph was one of her family, hanging on the wall in a gilded frame.

Stop procrastinating.

As Enrique pulled the ring box from his jacket pocket, his hand trembled. He didn't know why since this was a mere formality, but he couldn't stop thinking something still could go wrong. "I thought tonight would be the perfect time to present you with an engagement ring."

He opened the velvet box. An elegant sapphire with diamonds around the sides sparkled.

She gasped. "It's gorgeous."

His tight shoulders relaxed. "The ring belonged to my great-great-grandmother."

"Did your mother wear this?" Madeleine asked, not taking her gaze from the ring.

"No." The word came out sharper than he intended. "My mother kept her engagement ring after the divorce."

"I'm sorry your parents split up. That had to be difficult."

He shrugged, but he didn't feel indifferent. He'd

been eight the last time he saw his mother, but he hadn't forgotten her even though he wished he could. She'd asked to take Alejandro with her when she left, but she hadn't wanted Enrique. She'd thought he was unable to love or be loved.

Like his father.

For as long as he remembered, his parents had fought, yelling and screaming while he and Alejandro hid in the secret tunnels beneath the palace until they felt it was safe to come out.

"It made me stronger." That was as much as he wanted to say for now. He forced a smile. "Tonight is our party, the first we'll attend as a couple. Let's focus on that and the future, not the past."

She nodded, but he didn't miss the sympathy in her gaze.

"I had only seen your photograph, but I picked this ring from our family's collection because of your eyes," he explained.

"That's so thoughtful." Madeleine extended her left hand. "I can't wait to see it on."

Enrique slid the band over her French manicure nails and onto her finger.

"It's a perfect fit." She sounded surprised but pleased.

That made him happy. "Your parents provided your size so I could have the band adjusted."

"Smart thinking."

He stood taller.

"I love it." Madeleine flexed her fingers. Her smile brightened her face. "Thank you."

Enrique took her hand, the one wearing his ring, and kissed the top of it. His lips wanted to linger against her soft skin.

She sucked in a breath but didn't pull away from him.

That didn't make what he was doing right. Not when he knew she continued to grieve Louie.

Enrique let go of her hand. "I am grateful you agreed to marry me. I will do all I can to see that you are happy on the island, and that our children know they are loved unconditionally."

Something he hadn't known until two years ago.

Madeleine's eyes twinkled. "I am thankful you want to marry me, Enrique. Our marriage may not be what either of us hoped for, but we will make the best of it."

Her genuine smile loosened something in his chest. She was correct. This wouldn't be a love match, but they would make this work for their countries, their children, and for themselves.

That would be enough.

Especially once he was king.

Madeleine recognized most of the guests at the engagement party. A band played, and people spoke above the music. She made her way from one group to another with Enrique at her side, greeting and accepting congratulations. The last time she'd seen most of them had been Louie's funeral.

Why were they here now?

Curiosity?

That had to be the reason.

The upcoming royal wedding was nothing more than a farce, given what a marriage should be. More than once she found herself reaching for Enrique's hand. For support, yes, but mainly because he was the only other person here who had an inkling of what she was feeling.

She could handle hearing "Best Wishes" and "Congratulations," but the "Enjoy the honeymoon," with an unsubtle nudge-nudge and "Are you planning to start a family right away?" disconcerted her. Okay, it made her queasy.

Heirs were required. That meant they would sleep together. But she hadn't known her future husband for a week yet. She wasn't ready to think about that part of their marriage. Saying "I do" would be difficult enough.

As Enrique spoke to a trade minister, Karl touched her shoulder. "It's time to open the dance floor."

Ugh. It didn't matter how much time had passed since she last had to do this. One thing hadn't changed.

The trade minister wished them well before rejoining his wife.

"Fair warning," she whispered in Enrique's ear.

"I've taken lessons, but I'm a horrible dancer."

"I'll take care of you." His voice was low, and his warm breath sent shivers along her spine. "Hold my hand."

She did with no hesitation.

As he led her onto the dance floor, her muscles tensed. She didn't need to look around to know everyone was watching them. She might be a princess, but she hated being the center of attention. That had been the biggest difference between her and Louie. He'd thrived on being in the spotlight. Craved it. Which was why when they'd been together, people watched him, not her. The last time she'd felt this exposed was at his funeral.

"Relax," Enrique mouthed. "It'll be fine."

All she could do was nod, but she wanted to believe him.

Music—a waltz—played. She nearly groaned, but before she could say anything, Enrique was leading her around the ballroom with the skill of a professional dancer. In his experienced hands, She floated across the parquet floor.

He was so handsome, the definition of suave and debonair. He moved as if he'd been dancing forever. His talent hid her flaws. The way he led made it easy for her to look as if she knew what she was doing. Funny, how he could be so awkward at some things and nail the others.

"How did you learn to dance so well?" she asked.

"We had a private instructor. My brother and I hated every minute, but our father forced us to take lessons into our teens. For our own good, he claimed."

Had his father pushed him to do other things, taking away time from Enrique's beloved garden? Given the way he'd reacted when his parents' divorce came up, she assumed the answer was yes. "Karl and I took lessons, too. But neither of us can dance like you."

Enrique beamed. "Then it was worth the trouble."

Her stomach fluttered. Nerves? Or something else?

He spun her around.

She laughed. "I may have to reconsider how I feel about dancing."

"Enjoying yourself?"

His smoldering gaze sent her heart racing. "Yes."

"Then we must keep dancing."

And they did.

Others joined them on the dance floor, but she barely noticed anyone else. Nor did she care who was watching. It was only her and Enrique. That was all that mattered.

"What are you thinking?" he asked.

"How nice this is," she admitted. "Thank you."

"For what?"

"Making being on the dance floor with you so easy."

His gaze narrowed. "Was it difficult before?"

"Not difficult. Different." That was the best way

to describe it. "Do you mind others watching us?"

"It's impossible to go unnoticed at an event like tonight when we're the guests of honor. I don't think about the people who might be staring. If I did, I'd miss a step or fall."

"If you do, I'll take full responsibility."

"As you should," he joked.

Enrique was the opposite of Louie, who with his blond hair and blue eyes lit up a room. Drew attention wherever he went. He didn't mind sharing the spotlight with her, but she let him have it.

Enrique appeared to do what was required of him with little regard to anyone else. He wasn't out to be the star. Though he didn't mind showing off. At least on the dance floor. Being with him like this was comfortable. He made it possible to ignore being center stage.

As the band announced a break, Enrique led her off the dance floor. He grabbed two flutes of champagne from a waiter's tray and handed her one. "Cheers."

She tapped her glass against his. The chime from the crystal meeting hung in the air. A perfect sound to mark the occasion.

He sipped. "I don't appear to be the fiancé your guests expected."

Most probably assumed her parents would find someone more like Louie. As if that person existed. "Doesn't matter what they think."

"A proper princess should care."

"I haven't for the past five years. I've been doing what I wanted. If I cared, I would have joined the land of the living before this."

Enrique stared at her with interest.

Heat flooded her face. Her fingers tightened around the champagne flute. "I said that aloud, didn't I?"

He nodded. "But there was nothing wrong with what you said. You needed time."

She still did. Too bad she wouldn't get it. "I suppose we should mingle."

"We are the guests of honor."

They spoke to more people. Enrique didn't say much beyond repeating a person's name and answering questions about this year's Med Cup, a sailing race held on his island. About his educational reform initiative. About him getting married in Gaullia.

Easy questions he had no difficulty answering. Thankfully.

A waiter replaced their empty glasses with full ones.

"Hey, bro," a male voice said from behind them.

She turned. A man with shoulder-length dark hair approached them. His coloring and features reminded her of Enrique. Only he wasn't wearing a bow tie or cummerbund with his tuxedo. He'd left the top buttons on his shirt undone. He held a beer bottle.

As if on cue, Enrique hugged the man. "What are

you doing here?"

"Jules thought we could stop by your party tonight and then visit Vernonia to see Izzy, Niko, and their kids. They'll be at your wedding, too, so we'll return to Gaullia with them next week." The attractive man, who she guessed was Enrique's younger brother, surveyed the ballroom. "Jules is around here somewhere. She must have recognized someone."

"I'm sure she knows many. Aliestle is next door to Gaullia," Enrique said.

Madeleine struggled to keep a smile on her face. Even though the two countries were neighbors, the royal families never mingled. King Alaric's choice because her father had issued invitations over the years. He'd wanted Karl to marry Julianna, but her father said no without giving a reason.

"Alejandro, I'd like to introduce Princess Madeleine of Gaullia, my fiancée."

The final word flowed easily from Enrique's lips. Hearing herself called that wasn't as jarring as Madeleine thought it would be.

He looked at her. "This is my younger brother, Alejandro."

"I've heard a lot about you," she said to the man.

"All lies," Alejandro joked. "Unless what he said was good, then it's all true."

The two brothers looked alike except Alejandro had a more carefree style and attitude. Attractive, but Enrique appealed to her more. "The majority was good, though he may have mentioned you were a troublemaker growing up."

Alejandro laughed. "I was the black sheep of the family, but I've settled down."

"Only after you met Jules." Enrique's smile deepened the corners of his eyes.

The result—breathtaking. Madeleine stared, mesmerized.

A gorgeous blonde ran up to Enrique and hugged him. "I love the new tuxedo."

His smile widened.

An unfamiliar burning sensation filled Madeleine's stomach. She forced herself to breathe.

He stepped back and motioned to her. "Jules, this is Madeleine."

The woman's face lit up. She was more beautiful in person and taller than expected.

"It's so wonderful to meet you." The princess from Aliestle took Madeleine's left hand in hers to examine the engagement ring. "The ring is beautiful. Excellent choice, Enrique."

He raised his glass to Jules. "Thanks."

She let go of Madeleine's hand. "I've never had a sister, so I can't wait to have a sister-in-law."

The words and expression on her face were so sincere and heartfelt, Madeleine swallowed around the unexpected lump of emotion. "It's a pleasure to meet you, Julianna. I've never had a sister, either."

"Please. Call me Jules." She tilted her head toward

Enrique. "It took this one a while to do that, but he's no longer as stuffy."

Enrique raised his head. "I was never stuffy."

"Yes, you were," Jules and Alejandro said at the same time and then laughed.

Enrique joined in.

Feeling like an outsider among the trio, Madeleine sipped her champagne.

"How about we take a walk?" Jules asked. "I'd love to hear about the wedding plans, and I'm sure these two want to catch up."

Madeleine glanced at Enrique.

"Go ahead," he said. "You've only discussed the wedding with me, your mother, and the planner."

That was true. Karl had been disinterested except for what signature cocktail would be offered during the reception. Still Madeleine hesitated. This was their engagement party, which meant they should probably stay together.

Enrique leaned closer. He smelled so good.

"You don't have to remain at my side," he whispered. "Go chat about all things bridal. Find me when you're finished. Alejandro will make sure I don't embarrass myself."

"Thank you." As she followed Jules, Madeleine glanced over her shoulder. Her gaze met his.

He smiled, a closed-mouth smile she'd seen before except this time her pulse sped up. A part of her wanted to go back and stay at his side.

Wait. That wasn't… She shouldn't feel…

Madeleine faced forward, walking away from Enrique and his brother.

The party and wedding talk must be getting to her. Oh, and her engagement ring. What else could have her feeling so weird?

Chapter Eight

Enrique watched Madeleine make her way to the other side of the ballroom. Fighting the urge to follow her, he forced his feet to remain in place. It wasn't easy.

He didn't know why he felt compelled to go with her because he wanted the two women to become friends. She would need someone besides him when she arrived on the island. Who better than Jules?

"She's beautiful," Alejandro said over the music that played again.

As Madeleine disappeared into the crowd, Enrique

turned toward his brother. "Jules is."

Alejandro snickered. "I meant your fiancée."

Oh. Enrique had been trying to ignore her appearance. For both their sakes. Seeing her dressed up tonight, however, had made that impossible to do. He wanted to keep dancing with her so he could hold her without it being…weird.

Alejandro laughed. "You're thinking about her now."

"Madeleine is beautiful." Enrique kept his voice steady. No emotion allowed. "I'm a fortunate man."

"A man who will be king given how well your engagement appears to be going."

"I've made a few mistakes, but Madeleine hasn't backed out yet." Enrique raised his champagne glass. "Here's to hoping she doesn't."

"I'll drink to that." Alejandro lifted his beer bottle.

Leave it to his rebel brother to bypass drinks in proper glasses, but Alejandro had always done what he wanted. Even as a child. Enrique smiled before taking a sip.

Alejandro motioned to the doors. "Let's talk outside where it's less crowded."

Enrique stepped onto the patio lit by old-fashioned-looking lampposts that belonged in Narnia. The quiet was a relief. Unlike his brother, he hadn't made a habit of going to clubs and parties. He preferred staying at home or working in his garden.

The sun had set two hours ago, but the

temperature remained warm. Thank goodness the ballroom was air-conditioned or guests would be complaining. He unbuttoned his tuxedo jacket to keep from sweating.

"I don't know how you do it," Alejandro said.

In the distance, Enrique glimpsed the broken fountain. He needed to have that fixed for Madeleine. Before they left for the island, if possible. "Do what?"

His brother waved his beer bottle in a circle over his head. "The crown prince gig. Dealing with idiots daily."

Enrique laughed. He knew what that meant. "You met with Parliament."

"Twice since you've been in Gaullia." Frustration edged each word. "The second visit was because they didn't listen the first time. I took Jules with me, so I had a witness."

"The robed fools—that's what Father calls them—can be challenging." Enrique sipped his champagne. "But Father usually handles them. Why were you there?"

"He was more tired than usual, so his doctor ran more tests. Nothing conclusive was found, but he's supposed to rest."

Enrique's chest squeezed tightly. He didn't want his father to work himself to a heart attack or worse. "Being the king is a tiring and thankless job. You can't please everyone."

"I offered to speak with the Parliament in Father's

behalf so he could take the day off. He asked me not to yell at them, and I didn't. Even though, I came close. More than once."

"You did better than me."

Alejandro raised a brow. "You yelled?"

Enrique nodded. "They deserved it."

"Over the new succession law?"

"No. I haven't been to the chamber since the new law went into effect." He'd purposely stayed away. "I can't remember what foolishness they were discussing when I yelled, but I was, shall we say, riled."

Laughter from the ballroom drifted out. Enrique hoped Madeleine was enjoying herself.

Alejandro stared at the sky. A crescent moon hung low as if painted there. He took another drink of his beer.

"What's on your mind?" Enrique asked. "You're never this quiet unless you're staring at Jules."

"It's just…" Alejandro dragged his hand through his hair. "Please do whatever it takes to marry Madeleine. I—"

The air rushed from Enrique's lungs. His insides twisted. "You promised you would take the throne if I can't."

"I will." The words flew out. "I won't go back on my word, but I don't want the throne. Two days of dealing with Parliament has been enough. If I must face that much stupidity daily, I'll go crazy."

Enrique's shoulders relaxed. This was nothing

more than growing pains. "I felt the same way at first. You get used to it."

"Not sure about that, bro." Alejandro took another pull from his bottle. "You have the temperament to be king. The skills. I… Just say 'I do' next Saturday, okay?"

"That's the plan. I'm trying hard not to mess up."

"Try harder."

Enrique laughed before downing the rest of his champagne.

Alejandro studied him. "You like her."

"What's not to like? She's intelligent, beautiful, and has yet to kick me to the curb," Enrique joked because he didn't think anyone had noticed his growing affection for her. "Of course, I like Madeleine."

"Is there a spark?" Alejandro asked.

"A spark?"

"When you kiss?"

Enrique blew out a breath. If only he could expel his attraction for Madeleine as easily. "We haven't kissed."

"Why not?"

So many reasons, but the biggest one was she didn't want his kisses. Enrique wasn't ready to admit that to anyone. "You and Jules say I come on too strong around women so I'm being more cautious with Madeleine."

"You have in the past," his brother agreed. "But if there's chemistry, the connection will bring you closer."

Enrique believed something was drawing them together. Probably wishful thinking. "I don't want to push her."

"One kiss," Alejandro urged. "What do you have to lose?"

"The throne."

"Okay, you've got me there." Alejandro rubbed his chin. "Romance her."

"We're not in a romantic relationship."

Nor would they be in one.

"You're marrying her and going on a honeymoon. You realize a stork doesn't deliver heirs."

"I know how it works, but you've made a huge jump from kissing to…" Enrique couldn't say the word.

"My mistake, but a little wooing could go a long way."

Unless she didn't want to be wooed. Given she didn't want a love match that could be the case. He didn't want to upset her. Been there, done that.

Enrique cringed. "The last time I tried to woo a woman, I was forcibly escorted out of the country. You'd think she would have told me she was deathly allergic to nuts."

"Death by chocolate."

"She had an epinephrine auto-injector handy," he countered, though the memory made him shudder. "I wanted to apologize, sent flowers and books by her favorite author, but she never wanted to see me again."

"You tried, but there isn't room for mistakes this time." Alejandro's serious tone was a reminder of what was at stake. "Have you asked Madeleine if she's allergic to anything?"

"No."

"Do that," Alejandro suggested. "Tonight."

"I've seen her eating chocolate, and she didn't mention being allergic to pollen when we were in the gardens. Which is a good thing since I sent her flowers before I arrived."

Alejandro grinned. "Nice touch."

"Jules suggested it." That reminded Enrique of something from when he and Jules were engaged. "Do you think I should ask Madeleine out on a date?"

"You're getting married. A date would be a great idea, but only if you'll feel comfortable. When you're under pressure—"

"I mess up."

Alejandro nodded. "Forget what you like to do. Plan an outing that she would consider romantic."

"Gee, thanks."

"Nothing personal but with your track record—"

Enrique held up his hand, cutting off his brother. "No need to explain."

"Set the mood while you're together so kissing her goodnight won't seem like a big deal."

Except it could be a huge deal to Madeleine. "What if she says no to the kiss?"

"Try again."

Enrique could, but he didn't want Madeleine to feel awkward or forced into something she didn't want. "We have plenty of time to figure this out."

Five years, to be exact.

For kisses and babies.

"Everything doesn't have to happen this week or even next month." Enrique wanted Madeleine to be comfortable with him. "We need to get to know each other better before we—"

"Get naked." Alejandro elbowed him. "Just kidding."

The joke didn't make Enrique feel better.

"All I'm saying is you and Madeleine should have a large family," Alejandro continued. "Your kids will be gorgeous. And father will love having grandchildren."

"You and Jules can do your part there."

"We're working up to it. Practice makes perfect. You'll see." Alejandro laughed. "This is one duty you'll find highly enjoyable."

Enrique's face heated. He raised his empty glass only to remember he'd drunk all the champagne.

"I expect to hear how the princess wooing is going." Alejandro's tone said he wasn't joking.

Great. More pressure. Enrique sighed. "I will ask Madeleine on a date, but I make no promises about kissing her."

Unless she makes the first move. He wouldn't turn down a kiss if she offered, but he had the feeling that wouldn't happen until they were standing at the altar and had been pronounced husband and wife.

Unfortunately.

"Your castle reminds me of ours in Aliestle. You may need time to adjust to living on La Isla de la Aurora." Jules waved to someone. "The island is a gorgeous place to live, but it's different from being inland and near the Alps."

"Enrique called it a vacation paradise." Madeleine peered over the crowd but didn't see him. Funny, but she felt more comfortable next to him. Maybe that was because she'd avoided events like this since the funeral. She hated the pity in people's eyes. Except their curiosity tonight wasn't much better.

"It is." Jules waved to someone else. "Do you sail?"

"No. I've never been."

"We can remedy that." Jules smiled at her. "The island is turning into a sailing mecca. They're building marinas and resorts. Alejandro owns a boatyard, and we both enjoy racing."

Sailing sounded windy with the chance of being sunburned, but maybe Madeleine didn't understand the appeal. "That's nice you share something in common."

"It helps, though my marriage to Alejandro wasn't arranged."

Unlike yours was implied.

Madeleine wasn't offended. Some royals were given the choice to marry for love. She had been the first time. "I'm sure Enrique and I will find a hobby or something to share."

"You will." Jules's voice was adamant. "Plus, you'll have children to raise together. I hope they have your blue eyes."

The darker blue of Louie's eyes, not hers. That was what Madeleine imagined when she thought of children. Blond hair, too. Only…

The room spun. Madeleine focused on the glass in her hand until the dizziness disappeared. "We haven't discussed children in detail."

Her real-life babies would probably have darker hair, brown eyes, and olive skin. Opposite of Louie and the children she'd dreamed of having for so long.

Jules's gaze narrowed. "I'm sure you'll talk about this eventually because Enrique wants a big family."

Madeleine gulped. She hoped two nights in his bed would end up in two pregnancies—an heir and a spare and that would be the extent of their physical relationship. Two children were enough. That was how many Louie had wanted.

Except she wasn't marrying Louie.

Frustration grew inside her. She had to stop comparing the two men. They were different—beyond one being dead and the other alive. So were her feelings for them—one was the love of her life and the other was saving her country.

She didn't want to think about any of that right now. "The wedding has been our focus."

"As it should be." Jules came closer. "Enrique is a good man. He tried to emulate his father to earn his respect. Imagine an eight-year-old boy wearing a suit every day. It's only been in the past two years, Enrique has come into his own, so to speak. You may need to be patient with him."

"He admitted having faults."

"Did he mention his workaholic tendencies?" Jules asked.

"No, but that seems to be a trait of some crown princes. Such as my brother."

"Not mine, unfortunately." Jules laughed. "But I haven't given up hope Brandt will change as he gets older. Enrique works hard, but having a wife will mean he needs to balance better."

"He has an important job. Long hours go with the title. I would never ask him to set aside his work." Madeleine appreciated Jules trying to help, but this would not be a typical marriage. "Enrique also has his garden, so I imagine his free time is limited."

Jules's eyes widened. "He told you about the garden?"

"Yes, and it appears he's been ignoring it because of his workload."

"He has." Jules glanced around. "Digging and planting are good for him. It may sound cliché or like a pun, but working in the garden grounds him. His relationship with his father was…strained until two years ago. He has had no contact with his mother since he was eight."

"He mentioned his parents divorced, but it appeared to be a sore subject. One he didn't want to discuss."

"Alejandro is the same way." Jules made a face like she'd bit into a lemon. "The split affected each brother differently. But both are desperate to be accepted for who they are and loved."

A rock settled in Madeleine's stomach. "He mentioned you said love could grow."

"It can." The words flew out of Jules's mouth. "And I'm so happy Enrique mentioned that to you. I hope that means he's willing to give it a chance to happen."

"Enrique sounded like he was." Except Madeleine had shot him down. Not that he'd appeared surprised. But it was better this way, so no one had unrealistic expectations about what might happen during the marriage. "He wants to make me happy."

Which meant love was off the table.

Jules's face brightened. "Enrique has changed so much since I met him over two years ago. Just remember whatever happens, he's trying his best. He may need encouragement or help or even a second chance."

"I understand." And Madeleine did. "I'm bringing my own baggage. We may need an additional luggage cart to carry his and mine into this marriage."

Jules laughed. "Besides patience, having a sense of humor is important. You'll fit in well."

Relief flowed through Madeleine. "I hope so, but the unknown is—"

"Nerve-racking. But you won't find yourself curtailed on the island. Women are treated as equals on La Isla de la Aurora."

Madeleine had heard about Aliestle's archaic ideas about gender and the lack of equality there. "Good to know they share modern views as Gaullia does."

Jules's lips parted. "You aren't being forced to marry Enrique?"

"My parents gave me the choice." Even if saying no wasn't an option because of King Alaric. Madeleine wondered if Jules knew what her father had threatened to do. "But I can't deny that marrying Enrique will be good for our country."

"And you'll be wonderful for the island."

Madeleine raised her chin. "Thank you."

"How are you and Enrique getting along?"

"Well enough given we've only known each other for a few days and will be married in a week." Saying that reminded her how quickly things were happening.

"I had four arranged matches—none of which made it to the altar—but none were scheduled to happen that fast."

She shrugged, but a part of her wished today had been their wedding and this their reception. If only to know Gaullia was safe. "The marriage contract has been signed. There's no reason to wait. Enrique has obligations on the island, and I can't see wasting months planning a wedding."

"Shhh." Jules feigned shock. "You'll give us princesses a bad name. Most people believe all we want to do is meet our Prince Charming, fall in love, get married in an elaborate spectacle, and have a little prince and princess."

That was all Madeleine had wanted with Louie. The pang in her heart deepened. She forced a laugh. "Don't forget conquering the villain before getting married."

"I'll let you in on a secret." Jules glanced around before leaning closer. "The villain to be conquered is inside us. But if you trust your heart, you'll win. True love always wins."

"Thanks for letting me in on the secret."

Madeleine could tell the woman believed that wholeheartedly, but she knew better. One thing the heart couldn't defeat was death. Though true love remained, so maybe that counted as a win and not a total loss.

Chapter Nine

After breakfast, Madeleine left Enrique in the dining room to spend time alone with his family. He'd wanted her to stay, but she needed a break.

Not from him.

Enrique had been nothing but sweet and attentive, including giving her a daisy when he joined them at the table. But the love flowing between Jules and Alejandro was palpable, reminding Madeleine of her and Louie.

Seeing it—them—hurt.

Because she missed that. Missed him. Missed having someone love her so much the thought of him not being with her made each breath a struggle.

Which it was.

The last thing she wanted to do was cry in front of her soon-to-be husband and in-laws, so she'd eaten quickly, said her goodbyes, and escaped to the parlor. If she'd retreated to her room, Mrs. Hobbs would have noticed and mentioned it to her parents. Madeleine didn't want them or anyone to worry about her.

She settled in her favorite chair. Her latest embroidery project was within arm's reach, but she studied her itinerary for the day instead. Today's list contained places to go regarding the wedding. The same as yesterday—except for one that read, *Date 7:00 PM.* She had no idea what that meant. Was it a placeholder for an event Mrs. Hobbs forgot to fill in?

"Here you are." Enrique entered the room. Handsome, dressed impeccably in a suit, but she wondered if he wore casual clothes like his brother, who'd been in shorts, a T-shirt, and sneakers. Maybe Enrique wasn't ready to let go of all the ways he emulated his father. "Alejandro and Julianna are off to Vernonia. They are excited to see the twin boys and meet the newest princess in the land."

Madeleine hoped this wouldn't turn into a talk about children. Her emotions were too fragile— threadbare and ready to break—to handle that.

Time to change the subject. "I enjoyed meeting your brother and sister-in-law."

Enrique sat across from her. "They like you. Jules

can't wait to teach you how to sail."

"She seems to enjoy it."

"Loves it. She's a world-class sailor who has won awards and may compete in the next Summer Games."

Madeleine leaned forward. "Really? Jules never mentioned that."

He laughed. "She's modest. Plus, she was more interested in talking about the wedding."

And discussing him.

Madeleine bit back a smile, wondering if he knew his sister-in-law was also his champion. "Jules will be a good friend to have."

"I agree." He rubbed his palms over his pants as if he was nervous. "Maybe you'll become best friends."

Madeleine considered that. "Karl wouldn't mind someone else taking over the position. I fear he's tired of it. Of *me*. Not that I blame him. I've wet his shoulder too many times with tears."

Enrique's brows drew together. "Karl is your best friend?"

She nodded, not adding that before her brother it had been Louie. "That's one reason there isn't a maid of honor for the wedding. Children of various cousins will be the attendants."

That had seemed the easiest solution to her lack of a close female friend to participate in the biggest event of her life. Asking an obscure relative hadn't appealed to her. Nor did she feel right asking Louie's older sister to be the matron of honor.

"Who is your best friend?" she asked.

Enrique tilted his head. "I'm not sure I've ever had one. Alejandro drew a crowd wherever he went, but it was always just me. As a child, I was either shadowing my father or the gardener. I had friends at boarding school and college, but I only see them occasionally. Usually when a visit coincides with business."

"Work keeps you busy."

"Jules mentioned that to you?"

"She did," Madeleine admitted.

"It's true. Alejandro handed over his responsibilities to me a few years ago, and now my father is preparing to retire so I've taken on more."

"You'll be prepared when you are king." She respected his dedication. "Please know, your work comes first. I will never hold doing your duty against you."

"Thank you." He leaned back on the sofa, more at ease than she'd seen him all morning.

"But try to spend more time in the garden, if you can," she added. "It might help you relax."

"I will." His eyes twinkled. "I have an idea that will help both of us relax tonight."

The hint of mystery in his voice intrigued her. She angled toward him. "What?"

"Have dinner with me."

Something fluttered in her stomach. "We eat dinner together every night."

"With your brother and parents," Enrique said

without missing a beat. "I meant the two of us. More like a date. Except without the, uh, romance part."

Date. She glanced at the piece of paper she'd been reading. "Is that what's listed on my itinerary?"

His face flushed. "I should have asked you before talking to Mrs. Hobbs, but I didn't want to disrupt your schedule." The words poured out like floodwaters through a spillway. "I'm sorry."

His uncertainty tugged at her heart. He was trying to make the most of their situation, and she appreciated that. She didn't expect or need a date, but turning him down wasn't an option. He was to be her husband and the father of her children. That meant she needed to get to know him better.

She smiled. "Having dinner with you would be lovely. We need time alone."

Relief filled his eyes. "We should be safe without our bodyguards hovering. I'll tell Captain Mendoza to keep his distance."

"I will tell mine the same thing." She wanted the dinner to go well. "Should I dress up?"

"No, wear something you'll be comfortable in. Not pajamas or yoga pants."

"So not hang-around-the-castle casual."

His eyebrows shot up. "Is that a style?"

She laughed. "No, but with a few phone calls, it could be."

"Jules's former maid, Yvette, works for a designer."

Enrique's earnest tone meant Madeleine wouldn't tell him she was joking. "I'll remember that."

His chest puffed. The look of pride on his face was adorable.

Jules had been correct. Enrique reminded Madeleine of a young boy, eager to please and desperate for praise. Thinking about his childhood hurt her heart. She wanted to help him heal. Friends did that for each other.

The silence between them wasn't uncomfortable. The quiet soothed her. But she wanted to know if he had free time this morning.

"I—" she said.

"Do—" he asked at the same time.

They both laughed.

"You first," he said.

"I have nothing scheduled for an hour. Would you like to take a stroll through the garden?"

As his eyes lit up, he stood. "Yes. But I have a conference call soon."

She rose to her feet. "We can fit it in."

"Excuse me, Your Highnesses." Mrs. Hobbs entered the room. The lines on her face were deeper and her lips pressed together. She opened her mouth, but no words came out.

Oh, no. This wasn't how the efficient woman who kept the castle and royal family in order acted. Madeleine rushed to her side. "Is there a problem?"

Mrs. Hobbs blinked. "A visitor wants to see Prince

Enrique in the foyer, ma'am. A child. From the hospital."

Enrique's face paled. His pulse ticked at his neck. He said nothing but walked out of the room, his heels clicking against the wood floor.

"Wait," Madeleine called after him.

"I must take care of this," he said, not turning around.

The regret in his voice slammed into her. She understood his wanting to handle this without delay, but she wanted to help him so he didn't make another mistake.

Or fail.

He, however, appeared intent on dealing with the child now.

Her anxiety swirled. She followed, quickening her pace to catch up with him. Mrs. Hobbs took up the rear.

Please don't let this go wrong.

In the foyer, a young boy stood with a determined expression. A soccer jersey hung on his thin frame. His shorts were baggy, too. A gust could blow him over. He clutched something in his right hand.

Next to him was a woman who appeared to be in her early thirties with dark circles under her eyes. She wore a sundress with a pair of sandals, but the bright colors only magnified her exhaustion. The poor woman needed a nap.

Enrique's posture was board stiff. He flexed his

fingers. "Someone is here to see me?"

"I'm sorry for the intrusion, Your Highnesses." The woman stifled a yawn. "My son has been asking to come to the castle since Prince Enrique's visit to the children's hospital. I finally relented and drove him here because he threatened to walk."

The boy raised his chin. His clenched knuckles turned white. "I could have made it."

"It's fine, and you would have," Enrique assured both. "Obviously, the visit must be important."

The boy nodded.

Madeleine had no idea why the child wanted to see Enrique. Given Mrs. Hobbs's worried expression, neither did she. But Enrique appeared ready to take whatever punishment he must for his behavior at the hospital. Madeleine's respect for him grew.

The boy stepped forward. No fear or hesitation in his eyes. "I'm Reginald Reimer. I'm ten years old, and you can call me Reggie."

Enrique acknowledged him with a nod. "I am Enrique Cierzo de Amanecer from La Isla de la Aurora."

Reggie stared up at him as if in awe. "The island of the dawn."

Enrique's gaze zeroed in on the boy. "Yes."

"I was at the hospital for a checkup when you visited." No judgment sounded in the boy's words. "My mom says some adults, even future kings, get scared at hospitals."

"Your mother is correct," Enrique said, his words clipped. "I was afraid."

The way his voice cracked hurt Madeleine's heart. She wanted to touch him so he would know he wasn't alone, but something held her back.

"Of germs?" Reggie asked.

"Yes," Enrique admitted. "I don't want to get sick."

"Me, either." Reggie covered his chest with his free hand. "I have a new heart. Germs can cause trouble."

"Sometimes the things we can't see frighten us the most," Enrique said.

Unable to stop herself, Madeleine rested her palm on Enrique's shoulder. A touch to let him know he wasn't alone.

He glanced at her.

The gratitude in his gaze nearly knocked her over.

"I heard you had to be alone at the hospital when you were a kid," Reggie said.

"That is true." If Enrique was trying to sound nonchalant, he was failing, but that only made the crown prince appear more human and approachable. She squeezed, another reminder she was here with him. "I was sick, but my family wasn't with me."

"I'm so sorry, sir. That must have been awful." Reggie's young face scrunched. "When I got my new heart, my parents never left me. I can't imagine how sad you were."

The compassion and empathy in the boy's voice brought tears to Madeleine's eyes.

"Thank you." Enrique's ramrod posture softened. "It was a long time ago."

The boy blew out a breath. "Still sucks."

"Reggie!" his mother chastised.

Reggie sighed, one that said *my mom has no idea what it's like.*

A grin tugged on the corners of Enrique's mouth. "It does suck. Which is why I want to stay healthy. So I don't have to go through that again."

"I feel the same way, sir." Reggie rewarded Enrique with a dazzling smile. One that added color to his face.

Even Enrique's stoic bodyguard, the watchful Captain Mendoza, appeared to be holding back a grin.

"I brought you something. In case you go back to the hospital to visit patients like me. It's small enough to fit in your pocket." Reggie handed something to Enrique. "Soap and water kills germs the best, but hand sanitizer works if there isn't a sink nearby."

Enrique focused on a clear bottle with a blue lid before looking at the child. "Thank you, Reggie."

"You're welcome, sir. I thought it might help you not be so scared of germs."

"This is thoughtful of you. Thank you."

The boy shrugged. "I like the puzzle you gave me. Though I haven't finished it. But I will."

"I appreciate your gift. I'll use it now." Enrique

flipped open the lid, squeezed a dollop of sanitizer onto his palm, tucked the small bottle into his jacket pocket, and rubbed his hands together. "May I shake your hand, Reggie?"

The boy's eyes widened. He extended his arm. "Yes, sir."

The two shook.

"Strong grip," Enrique said.

Reggie beamed. "I've been getting stronger each day."

"Keep it up."

"I will."

Enrique's gaze bounced from the boy to his mother and then to Madeleine. "The princess and I are taking a short walk through the garden. Would you like to come with us? Your mother can stay here and enjoy a few moments to herself."

Reggie seemed to grow inches taller. "May I, Mother?"

"Yes, a few minutes to myself would be nice, but no touching dirt," she warned her son, her voice going from soft to firm.

"Thanks, Mom."

"Is Reggie allowed to touch flowers?" Enrique asked her.

"That is fine, sir," she said. "But he can't move as fast as he thinks he can. Not yet anyway."

Madeleine hoped that changed soon for Reggie,

but she didn't know how long it took a transplant patient to recover.

"We'll be careful. I promise." Enrique glanced at Mrs. Hobbs. "Please adjust my schedule as necessary."

Madeleine's heart melted. He must mean his conference call.

Mrs. Hobbs appeared almost giddy. "Of course, sir."

Madeleine had no idea what Enrique had in mind with this walk, but she was eager to find out. She realized her hand was still on him, so she lowered her arm to her side.

"Oh, and, Mrs. Hobbs, can you please take Reggie's mother to a quiet place where she can relax and bring her a cup of tea? Some cookies, too." He touched Reggie's thin shoulder. "Are you allowed to eat cookies?"

Reggie shook his head enthusiastically. "On special occasions and in moderation."

"I believe this counts as a special occasion. We'll make sure there are enough cookies for when we return." Enrique flashed Madeleine a mischievous grin. "How does that sound to you, my princess?"

Her heart thudded. "Absolutely perfect."

Just like the way he handled Reggie.

With a sigh, she followed the two to the garden.

Chapter Ten

"Bees are so interesting." As Reggie explained his fascination with the flying insects, he walked between Enrique and Madeleine. The boy found wonder in everything—from a rosebud opening to a bird flying overhead.

Enrique envied that ability. Alejandro had been the same way as a child.

"Each bee has a job to keep the hive going." Reggie stopped to sniff a rose. "I'd like to work with a beekeeper to learn more about them. But my mom said it's too dangerous."

"Because of your heart?" Enrique asked.

"A combination of things," Reggie said in a matter-of-fact tone. "I take medicine for my heart and have to be careful, but I'm allergic to bees. I told my mom not everyone gets stung. She still said no."

"Mothers worry," Madeleine explained. "I'm older than you, but mine still watches out for me. That's just how moms are. They can't help it."

"I should stop asking her, then." A thoughtful expression formed on the boy's face. "My mom worries about me because of my transplant. I could have died without a new heart. I should wait to do anything with bees until I'm older and can decide for myself."

"Smart thinking." Reggie impressed Enrique. The boy seemed older than his years, but perhaps what he'd been through with his heart made the difference. "You may change your mind about bees, too."

Reggie nodded. "I should think about it. I wouldn't want to do something stupid."

Enrique didn't understand. "Wanting to learn more about something isn't stupid."

"No, but I need to remember I have my new heart because someone else died. Their family must miss them a lot. I have to take care of myself so that person didn't die for nothing." Reggie's mouth gaped. "Look, a caterpillar."

The boy rushed a short distance ahead of them to examine it.

Madeleine laughed. "He's half puppy and half old soul."

"He is. The transplant…" Enrique stopped.

"Enrique?" she asked.

"Something Reggie said about his heart sparked a memory." Enrique watched the boy, who examined the caterpillar as if he were a biologist. "I wanted one."

"Wanted what?"

"A new heart." The memory was as vivid as the sun in the sky above them. "Before my mother left the island, I overheard her talking to my father. She said I was exactly like him. That my heart was as broken and incapable of loving as his was."

"I'm so sorry." Madeleine placed her hand on Enrique's arm. Her touch was gentle and what he needed. "What she told him was wrong. She must have been angry. Trying to hurt your father the way she was hurting."

Enrique nodded. "I've come to understand that emotion was at play, but I was only eight and believed her."

"Of course you did." Compassion, not pity, shone in Madeleine's gaze. "She was your mother. You had no reason not to believe her."

He appreciated that. "I didn't know I'd internalized that until two years ago."

"Words can be more damaging than fists."

"True."

His father threatening to give the throne to

Alejandro if Enrique didn't follow orders had been another life-changing moment. The irony he might be forced to walk away from his birthright to save the monarchy wasn't lost on him.

"Replacing my heart with a new one made perfect sense at the time. I wasn't nervous when I asked my father for a transplant. When he asked why, I told him my heart was incapable of loving." Enrique shook his head. "He laughed at me. Said only an idiot would want to replace a healthy heart. Told me to grow up because love only existed in books and movies. So I never mentioned it again."

"Not all fathers are like that. He should have listened to you. Dug deeper about why you felt that way."

"I buried what happened," Enrique admitted. "I only remembered because of a conversation with Jules. Ever since I told her what my mother said, other parts have surfaced."

"Thank you for sharing this." Madeleine squeezed his arm. "You can't change what your parents said, but how you deal with the past is under your control."

Enrique nodded. He appreciated hearing her say that.

Madeleine put her palm on his chest. "Do you know what I feel?"

The hammering heart of a fool who wants to fall in love.

Emotion clogged his throat. Enrique swallowed so he could speak. "What?"

"The heart of a kind and loving man. The strong and steady beat isn't telling me that. It's the way Jules talks about you. Your interaction with Reggie and his mother. How understanding you are with me. All of those things show your heart isn't broken. They prove your mother couldn't see how special you are. That's her loss, not yours."

His heart rate accelerated. He waited for Madeleine to lower her hand. She didn't. "Thank you."

"You're welcome."

Her gaze held his. He wanted them to become friends, and this told him they were on their way, if not already there.

"You have to see this, Your Highnesses." Reggie pointed to the ground. "There are two caterpillars."

"Come on." Madeleine lowered her hand, taking Enrique's in hers. "Seeing two caterpillars is so much better than one."

Her hand was smaller but fit with his perfectly. Warmth spread inside him. His heart continued to pound, not from excitement, but something unfamiliar.

He let her lead him to the boy, who grinned from ear to ear.

"I wonder when they'll become butterflies. I bet they'll be beautiful," Reggie said wistfully.

"They will." Enrique reluctantly let go of Madeleine's hand to move closer to Reggie. He touched the boy's narrow shoulder. The kid was all bone. "They may live in this garden when that happens.

Or perhaps nearby."

Reggie's face lit up as if a spotlight were shining on him. "That would be cool."

Enrique laughed. "Later this summer, when you see a butterfly, remember these two caterpillars. You never know, it could be one of them."

"I will, sir." The boy tilted his head. "Maybe I should learn more about butterflies since they don't sting and I'm not allergic. That way my mom won't worry so much."

"That sounds like an excellent idea." Enrique gave his handkerchief to Reggie. "Wipe your hands with this, and then you can clean them with my sanitizer."

"I didn't touch the caterpillars."

"No, but you've been touching plants." Enrique kept his voice low and steady. "It's better to be safe than sorry."

"Oh, right." Reggie cleaned his hands and then held out the square of white linen. "Here you go, sir."

"Keep it." Enrique opened the lid on the bottle. "Every man needs a proper handkerchief."

The boy's jaw dropped. "Wow. This is almost better than the puzzle."

Madeleine covered her mouth. With the sun behind her, she reminded him of an angel, complete with a glowing halo.

Smiling at her, Enrique bit back a laugh. "Almost."

Reggie placed the handkerchief in his shorts pocket and stuck out his hands for the sanitizer. "Is it time for cookies now, Your Highnesses?"

Enrique's gaze met Madeleine's again. He smiled at her, thankful for Reggie's visit and this walk with the two of them. "It's time."

As the hour for the date with Madeleine approached, Enrique second-guessed his plans. This morning he'd been certain of the dinner arrangements he'd made, but doubts filled him. Should he have picked a fancier place with five-star ratings from foodies?

Sweat dampened the back of his neck. Enrique glanced at his watch. It was too late to change plans now. He hoped she enjoyed his original idea.

Dressed in a pair of tan pants, a short-sleeved button-down shirt, and boat shoes, he knocked on her bedroom door.

She opened it. "Hi."

He found himself speechless. Madeleine was…beautiful. Her hair was pulled into a ponytail. She wore a cropped shirt, navy capris, and strappy sandals. He hadn't seen her since they said goodbye to Reggie and his mother, but it had been worth the wait.

She squinted. "You're not wearing a suit."

"I said casual dress."

"I know, but…" A charming pink colored her face. "I assumed you'd wear a suit, but you look good out of one. I mean, what you have on is great."

Seeing the princess flustered was more fun than it should be.

"You're lovely, as usual." And shorter, since she wasn't wearing heels, but he thought better of saying that. He bent his arm before extending it. "Shall we?"

Fifteen minutes later, the limousine parked in front of a small café. The window shades were drawn and a sign read *closed*, but a light shone through the glass door.

Madeleine peered through the limousine's side window. "This is a charming restaurant, but I believe they only serve breakfast and lunch."

"Tonight they will serve dinner." Karl had suggested the café to Enrique as a place they could eat in private.

His bodyguard sprang from the car and walked into the café despite what the sign said. Less than a minute later, he returned to the limo and opened the rear door. "They are ready for you, Your Highnesses."

Two minutes later, Madeleine entered first.

Enrique followed her.

The awed expression on her face was all he needed to see. "It's so lovely."

Lit candles sat on flat surfaces around the café. The flickering flames provided a warm glow. It would be the perfect romantic atmosphere for a couple about to embark on their forever. Enrique hoped it wasn't too much.

A white linen cloth covered a round table with two

chairs. Votives sat on either side of a clear jar filled with freshly cut daisies.

She glanced around. "There's only one table set."

"We're the only customers dining here tonight."

Her lips parted. "You went to so much trouble."

"No trouble. I only had to make a phone call to the owner for the dinner to come together."

She touched her throat before motioning to the table. "There are daisies."

Her surprise warmed his heart. "Did you think I'd forget?"

"No," she admitted. "But I wasn't expecting all this. Any of it, really. Thank you."

He pulled out a chair for her. "Please sit."

She did, and he moved to his seat.

"I had no idea you could reserve the entire café." Madeleine glanced around. "How did you know that?"

"It was Karl's suggestion. Your brother thought they might be open to a private dinner, so I called and asked."

A server dressed in white entered from the kitchen. He was young, early twenties, and his hair was a mix of bleach blond and rainbow colors.

"Good evening, Your Highnesses." He greeted them with a smile before placing glasses of water in front of them. "My name is Adrian. Tonight, we will serve you a special menu."

Enrique tried not to stare at Madeleine, but his gaze kept returning to her. He focused on Adrian.

"Thank you."

"I'll be back with your first course."

Madeleine leaned over the table. "I'm used to having quiche or a soup and salad combination here. I had no idea they served fancier food."

Knots formed in his chest. "Tonight won't be fancy. I asked for fun, casual dishes."

She covered his hand with hers. "That sounds wonderful. I need more fun in my life and in my stomach."

His breath came easier. The knots lessened. "Karl told me your favorites. I made a list of those and added mine. The final menu choice is the chef's, so I don't know what we're having."

"This will be *fun*."

As he stared at her hands—her nails neatly trimmed and painted—he hoped the evening went well.

Adrian carried a plate covered with small pie-shaped items and a bottle of wine. "Macaroni and cheese bites paired with a Chianti."

Her eyes sparkled. "I haven't had macaroni and cheese in years. Our former chef had the best recipe, but he retired."

Madeleine's smile pleased Enrique. "Try one."

She lifted her hand from his and did, sighing as if savoring the taste. "Delicious."

He raised his wineglass. "To good food and excellent company."

"And caterpillars that turn into beautiful butterflies."

Gazing into her eyes, Enrique tapped his glass against hers and then drank.

After taking a sip, she set her wineglass on the table before taking an appetizer. "Did Mrs. Hobbs reschedule your conference call?"

"Yes." He hated how tired his father had sounded. "I may have some work to do over the next few days."

"That's fine. Only a couple wedding details need to be sorted."

"Mrs. Hobbs mentioned the cake."

Madeleine wiped her mouth with a napkin. "The baker requested we do a tasting on site. It'll be good publicity for the shop if the press is there."

"At least we get to eat cake."

She grinned. "That will make it worthwhile."

"Especially if it's chocolate."

"Oh, the florist is including daisies in my bouquet. He's also adding them to several of the floral arrangements." She raised her wineglass. "Thank you for taking care of that."

"It was the least I could do. I haven't had to do much for this wedding other than show up when requested."

"Were you more involved…"

"In my wedding to Jules that never happened?" He half laughed. "Yes, but my ego made all the decisions. Having King Alaric footing the bill led me astray before

I knew what was happening. I learned I'm not a good wedding planner, and I know nothing about bridal wear."

"Do I want to know?"

Remembering the monstrosity of a wedding dress he'd had commissioned and wanted Jules to wear made him grimace. Enrique took a sip to wash away the sour taste in his mouth. "No. A bride is better off choosing what she wears than relying on me."

She stared at the flowers on the table.

"Is your gown ready?" he asked.

"I have a final fitting left to do."

Madeleine didn't sound excited. Why should she? This wasn't a marriage of her choosing. Nor was this her first wedding dress.

"I'm sure the gown will be perfect for you." Not that it mattered whether or not he liked what she wore. They could marry in a civil ceremony at the town hall dressed in sweatpants and T-shirts. "My colorful sash and ribbons will make me appear more like a cartoon prince."

She laughed. "It won't be that bad."

"I prefer a tuxedo, but protocol demands the uniform."

"The pains of being a royal."

"Yes, but I don't mind," he admitted. "If I wasn't a prince, I wouldn't be sitting here with you."

And there was nowhere in the world where he'd rather be than with Madeleine.

Chapter Eleven

The next morning, Madeleine paced in the cathedral's vestibule, waiting for the wedding coordinator, who was talking to the organist about the processional music. Anticipation made standing still impossible. She kept moving around, eager to walk down the aisle at this first of two rehearsals. But she didn't know why.

Maybe she wanted to cross the wedding items off her agenda. Whatever the reason for being so fidgety, she was losing patience. At least none of the page boys and flower girls were here. They would practice the day before the big event. She imagined the havoc bored children would have brought today.

Madeleine glanced at the altar. The wedding coordinator was still missing, but Enrique and Karl spoke to the bishop, who would perform the marriage ceremony. The three men laughed.

Even from this distance, she distinguished Enrique's laughter. The sound was deeper—richer—and something she enjoyed hearing.

The doors behind her opened. Her mother strolled inside, the familiar scent of her designer perfume wafting around her. She wore a bright green suit that matched her hat, purse, and shoes. "Have I missed anything?"

Of course, she would never apologize for being late. Her schedule took precedence over everyone else's, including the king's.

"Just waiting to walk down the aisle," Madeleine explained. "The organist played the wrong music, so the wedding coordinator is dealing with that."

Enrique glanced Madeleine's way, and his smile widened. He waved.

As her heartbeat quickened, she waved back.

"Your fiancé appears happy to see you," her mother said.

"We haven't seen each other today." Not since last night when he'd escorted Madeleine to her room after their date. As they'd stood at her door, she'd thought he would kiss her, but he didn't. He'd said goodnight like a gentleman.

She'd been…relieved. The twinge of disappointment was only because a kiss had seemed the proper way to end their wonderful evening together.

Her mother's gaze narrowed. "Karl told me Enrique went to a lot of effort for your dinner last night."

"He did." Happiness spread through Madeleine's body. "He booked an entire café for us. The owner, who is also the chef, decorated the interior with white candles and daisies and prepared a custom menu for us."

"That sounds charming."

"It was." Laughter bubbled inside her. She'd loved everything about the dinner. From the atmosphere to the food. The bacon cheeseburger with a side of French fries had been unexpected but delicious. The chocolate milkshakes topped with whipped cream, fudge sauce, and a cherry put any other beverage pairing to shame. "The chef served our favorite foods. Not fancy dishes, fun ones."

"You enjoyed yourself." Her mother sounded relieved.

"I did." Madeleine's gaze zeroed in on Enrique. "He surprised me."

"It's about time someone did." Her mother wrapped her arm around Madeleine in a half hug. "I'm so happy that you and Enrique are getting along."

"Me, too. He's sweet," Madeleine admitted. Today,

she'd found herself randomly wondering what he was doing. "Not horrible like I imagined he would be."

Her mother's eyebrows rose. "So he's no longer an ogre?"

Madeleine flinched. "I never called him that."

"Must have been your brother." Her mother stared at the altar. "Though Enrique never seemed that way to me. He strikes me as more of a Frog Prince."

"Except he hasn't been kissed by this princess," Madeleine joked.

Her mother tsked. "I told you to kiss him the first day."

"There hasn't been an opportunity."

Other than last night. Or when they'd danced at the engagement party. But taking the initiative hadn't occurred to her. Maybe she should—

Wait. She didn't want to kiss him, did she?

No. That wasn't possible.

They were friends. Friends who would marry in less than a week.

"You shouldn't put off kissing him," her mother urged. "Your marriage is critical to Gaullia's survival. This union will also secure your future. There are no negatives to the match. Stop holding yourself back."

"We just met. We're not in love." Her parents hadn't loved each other at first, but her mother must have forgotten that. "But no one is backing out."

At least not Madeleine. She couldn't speak for Enrique.

"That's a relief, but remember, your wedding is only the first day in your new life with your husband," her mother said. "You have specific duties to fulfill as his wife and his queen."

"You mean his princess," Madeleine corrected. "His father is king."

"Not for long." Excitement flashed in her mother's eyes. "The coronation ceremony planning is underway."

Enrique hadn't mentioned that to her. Not that it mattered. His being king wasn't the reason her parents secured this match. Still, her mother appeared delighted with the new timeframe. "I am prepared to help Enrique however I can."

"Excellent because he'll need you to listen and take care of him. The transition from one ruler to another can be difficult under the best of circumstances."

She remembered Enrique had mentioned his increased workload. "The transition may have started."

"Your goal will be to see that all his needs are met. Emotional and physical."

Emotional ones would be easy for Madeleine. The connection between her and Enrique drew them closer each day. But the other…

"I am to provide heirs, but—"

Lines tightened around her mother's mouth. "This won't be a one and done, Madeleine."

Jules's friend Izzy had given birth to twin boys. The princess of Vernonia also had a baby girl, and they wanted more children. But she and her husband, Crown Prince Niko, were in love, according to Jules.

Madeleine bit the inside of her cheek. "An heir and a spare are necessary. Beyond that—"

"Do you want to send your husband into the arms of a mistress? Raise children on your own? Or have another woman be viewed as 'mother' and part of the family?"

A shiver ran along Madeleine's spine.

"I haven't considered what a state marriage would entail except for us living separate lives." *Or what a divorce would mean long-term.* She balled her hands. "But you make it sound like my role as his wife is to only satisfy his needs."

Her mother studied Madeleine. "You know what's expected."

In theory, yes. But hearing it now… "Why didn't you mention this when I was marrying Louie?"

"There was no need." Her mother's gaze softened. "You loved Louie so much you would have done anything for him. The same as he would have done for you. You took care of each other like husband and wife from the time you were teenagers. The hardest thing was having you wait until you graduated to marry."

A familiar lump burned in Madeleine's throat. "I wish we hadn't waited."

Her biggest regret was not eloping as they'd joked about for years. If they'd married when she turned eighteen, they might have had a family—a child to keep

Louie's legacy alive.

Madeleine's eyes stung. She blinked.

Her mother squeezed her shoulder. "We did what we thought best for the two of you. For your future. No one knew what would happen to him, sweetheart."

Madeleine swallowed. Nodded. Took a deep breath to quiet the grief welling inside her.

"Enrique isn't Louie. Two men couldn't be more different, but he's trying to show you he cares and wants to make the marriage work," her mother said. "That much is clear to your father and me."

She cleared her throat. "We've become friends."

"Good. That's the first step." Her mother lowered her arm. "Enrique is a fine man. He'll be a strong ruler. No matter how you feel about him, you must support your husband in all ways."

Madeleine had prepared her entire life to be the support system of a crown prince and then a king. Funny, how that was the only thing she wanted to do when the man was Louie. Then again, she'd been young and in love and had thought little beyond living happily ever after.

"You like Enrique more than you thought you would. Get to know him better," her mother counseled. "You may come to care for him more. Fall in love."

Every muscle tensed. "No. I can't fall in love. Louie—"

"Isn't here." Her mother hugged her, the

unexpected show of emotion stealing Madeleine's breath. "You still miss him so much. But he would want you to live, laugh, fall in love again. Not spend the rest of your life in mourning, wishing he were still with you."

Not wanting to let go, she clung to her mother. "It's so hard."

"I wish I could make the hurt go away." Her mother squeezed her tightly. "Nothing can change your love for him. But don't let the memory of Louie stop you from living and loving again."

Madeleine stepped away. "Enrique and I aren't—"

"You just met. I'm not asking you to fall in love with him today, but open yourself and your heart to the possibility. You never know what might happen."

She nearly laughed. Falling in love again would be impossible. But appeasing her mother wouldn't hurt anyone. "I can try."

Even though Madeleine had no doubt she would fail.

Strains of Handel's "Overture" from "Occasional Overture" filled the cathedral. Enrique faced the rows of empty pews. More than one thousand guests were expected to attend the wedding. A film crew would televise the ceremony in Gaullia and La Isla de la Aurora.

Madeleine stood at the entrance to the church with her hands clasped in front of her. Her pink suit and nude pumps were nothing short of princess perfection, but he easily pictured her in a white gown and veil.

She would be a beautiful bride.

And he was the most fortunate of men because she was to marry him.

As she came closer, he noticed her smile. No teeth showed. It reminded him of the day they'd first met. He hadn't expected her to bounce with excitement, but her expression appeared forced. That concerned him after how comfortable she'd seemed last night.

Conversation and laughter had flowed smoothly. The only moment of tension had been saying goodnight. He'd wanted to kiss her. For a second, he thought she'd wanted that, too. But he'd remembered what she'd said about not wanting a love match and had drawn back. Doing so had taken every ounce of his willpower. But seeing her now…

Had the queen said something to upset Madeleine?

He hoped not.

Remembering his part, he stepped forward to take her hand.

When he touched her, a spark zinged. Must be static electricity.

Enrique escorted her to the altar. Awareness buzzed through him, or that might be nerves.

The music stopped.

The bishop, an older man with a receding hairline

and wire-rimmed glasses, acknowledged them with a gentle smile. He held a pen and a piece of paper. "Once the two of you are in position, I'll greet everyone. There will be an opening prayer and a song. A reading and a psalm will follow. Next come the vows. We'll go over them now."

As Enrique repeated the words and his sense of duty kicked into high gear, his nerves disappeared. This might only be a rehearsal, but he was one step closer to his goal. By marrying, his dream of ruling the kingdom would come true.

Madeleine was the catalyst. He owed her.

The urge to glance her way was strong, the desire to hold her hand stronger, but he kept his hands at his sides and focused on the bishop.

The man adjusted his glasses. "Who is providing the rings?"

"My brother, Alejandro," Enrique said. "He is the best man and will attend the next rehearsal."

The bishop wrote on the paper he held. "After the exchange of rings, a candle-lighting and another song will follow. Then you'll be pronounced husband and wife, and you can kiss the bride."

"Practice the kiss now," the queen announced from the aisle. "More people will be at the next rehearsal, so this is the best time."

"Go ahead," the bishop said.

Madeleine gazed up at Enrique. The corners of her mouth curved upward slightly. Not enough to be considered a smile. "It's fine."

"If you're sure…" he asked.

"I am."

This was about as unromantic a first kiss—or any kiss—as Enrique could imagine. Which was par for the course for him.

He nearly laughed.

Feeling unsure and on display, both things he hated, Enrique lowered his head. The floral-citrus scent of her wafted between them. He touched his mouth to hers. Another spark prickled but not as sharp as the first from their hands.

A little hesitant, he pressed his lips gently against hers. They were soft as he imagined but sweeter.

So sweet, one taste would never be enough. He wanted to feast on her kiss, but he feared slobbering all over her, so he held back, maintaining a light touch. He let his mouth linger longer than it should.

She wasn't looking for a love match. She wasn't interested in his kiss. But standing like this, his lips against hers, he'd found what had been missing.

His heart.

And home.

It wasn't the palace or the garden but the woman—the princess—right here.

He would be happy to keep kissing her forever, but he couldn't…

Couldn't push. Couldn't get carried away. Couldn't let her discover what he was feeling.

Enrique drew back, knowing that was for the best.

She grabbed on to his jacket lapels, pulled him closer, and deepened the kiss.

The way he'd wanted to do but hadn't.

There was no more uncertainty. Any tentativeness disappeared. This was needy and greedy and…

Heat balled in his gut. Sensations rocketed through him, exploding like fireworks. Nothing had ever felt so right, so wonderful.

Someone cleared his throat.

Madeleine jerked away, letting go of him.

"Oh, no," she mumbled, quiet enough Enrique doubted the bishop even heard her.

Karl laughed. "Not so proper a kiss."

Madeleine's face was flushed and her lips swollen. Her breathing came in puffs, the same as his. She looked at Enrique, regret in her eyes, before staring at the ground.

Kissing her had sent him flying, soaring through the sky like an Eleonora's falcon above his island. Her reaction now, however, sent him plummeting. He needed to say something, but emotion clogged his throat. He was torn between thanking her and apologizing.

"I see there will be no issues with the kiss." The queen sounded amused. "Thank you for humoring me."

Enrique didn't find the situation funny. Not when Madeleine wouldn't meet his gaze. Her hands trembled. Red stained her cheeks.

All he wanted to do was put a smile back on her face. He also wanted to kiss her again.

Not what she needed, but he had no idea kisses could be so addictive. He wanted another taste of the rightness, the sense of home, he'd found with her.

"Is there anything else you need from us?" Enrique asked the bishop.

"No, sir, you're finished."

Madeleine blew out a breath. She still hadn't looked up. Her words from the day they'd met echoed through his brain.

After Louie's death, I knew an arranged marriage awaited me. I also know heirs are expected, but I'm not looking for…

A love match.

I hope you understand. It's not you.

She'd been honest about what she wanted and didn't want.

He'd forgotten that.

The queen had pushed them into this kiss. He'd enjoyed every second, more than he should, and that was wrong.

Enrique might want a repeat the next time he stood at the altar, but this had been a mistake. One he needed to fix or there might not be a wedding. "I'm sorry."

Not that he was sorry for kissing her. He was sorry for not standing up to her mother, for upsetting Madeleine, for not being a man she could fall in love with.

But he would do everything he could to be a better man.

One who would make sure she was happy with their marriage and with him.

Chapter Twelve

Hands trembling, Madeleine hurried away from the altar, unable to speak. Her eyes stung, but no tears fell.

Yet.

She needed to make a quick escape and return to the palace where she could fall apart in private. She exited the cathedral.

On the steps, the sun beat down on her—the hot temperature a jolt from the cooler air inside. A glance at the street showed three limousines with royal flags on the hoods.

People passed by on the sidewalk, life going on as normal.

Not hers.

Everything seemed to have changed with one kiss.

That shouldn't be possible, yet…

Making her way to the first limo, Madeleine touched her tingling lips.

She was reeling from her response to Enrique's kiss.

Her driver opened the rear door, so she slid into the limousine.

Why did I kiss him back?

The question hammered in her brain.

His kiss had been chaste, a light touch of lips, a tad more than a peck, but that hadn't been enough.

Not for her.

What was I thinking?

Grabbing him, pressing her mouth harder against his, and not letting go.

She had done that.

In front of her mother, brother, the bishop, and the wedding coordinator. Had the organist seen, too?

Worse, Madeleine's lips wanted more kisses. But she shouldn't. Couldn't.

Guilt, thick and bitter, coated her throat as if she'd cheated on Louie.

His kisses had made her feel treasured, desired, and loved. She'd never imagined feeling that way again.

But Enrique's kiss had curled her toes. Sent her

heart pounding so much it might have burst out of her chest. Caused tingles to explode across her skin. Made her blood simmer.

"Ugh." Madeleine buried her face in her trembling hands.

Someone sat on the seat next to her. The familiar scent of aftershave tickled her nose.

Enrique.

Her nerve endings stiffened. She wanted to flee except there was nowhere to go.

Be the princess you were born to be.

She lowered her hands, straightening her posture, trying to pull herself together. His forearm rested in the space he'd left between them. That flight response kicked in again. She fought the urge to scoot away from him, but this wasn't his fault. He was doing everything right. She was the one to blame for what happened inside the cathedral.

Her.

Not him.

Which made her feel worse.

The limo door closed. The sound a reminder she was stuck in this small space with the man who, with a touch of his lips, had made her come alive and forget everything.

Breathe.

Keep breathing.

Less than a minute later, the vehicle pulled away from the curb.

Inhale. Exhale.
That's easy enough.
The limousine's privacy divider would keep anyone in the front from eavesdropping. Not that she knew what to say to Enrique.

Words failed her. Thoughts, too.

She shot him a sideway glance.

He was staring at her. "I wish I hadn't…"

The regret in his voice sliced into Madeleine. Her fingernails dug into her palms.

"You did nothing wrong." She sounded raw, unnatural, matching the way she felt.

"I kissed you," he countered.

As he'd brought his lips to hers, tenderly as if she were a cherished heirloom, something deep inside her had awakened. A part of her she thought had died with Louie.

Her heart.

It had roared to life—hungry and wanting more.

Everything Enrique was willing to give.

Her pulse skittered, and her cheeks flamed.

"I told you it was okay to kiss me. And I kissed you back." Oh, how she'd kissed him. "I'm the one who needs to apologize. I haven't…I usually don't…"

"Am I the first man you've kissed since Louie?" he asked softly.

"No. I've had a couple pecks after dates arranged by my family, but I never wanted…more."
Until now.

Enrique's innocent kiss had created a yearning for something she didn't understand. She fought the urge to wipe her mouth, as if that would make her forget the feel of his lips against hers and the way he tasted.

Enrique rubbed his temples. "I should have said something to your mother, but I didn't want to appear disrespectful."

"Nothing would have made a difference." Madeleine wanted to reach out and comfort him, but she didn't dare, because a touch might not be enough. Instead, she placed her right hand on the seat. "My mother has been wanting me to kiss you since the day you arrived."

Lines creased his forehead. "Why?"

"To seal the deal." Madeleine cringed, thinking of what might have happened had she followed the advice the first time. "Her words, not mine."

He shook his head. "We signed the contract."

"This was before that." The loan with Aliestle hadn't been disclosed during the marriage negotiations. This wasn't the time to bring that up. "They want our match to happen." *Desperately.*

"So do I." His hand scooted closer to hers, cutting the space between them in half but leaving a small gap. "I'm committed to marrying you."

His words cut into her. People called her proper, but her reaction to Enrique showed that she was a fraud.

"Thanks, but you deserve"—she rubbed her eyes

to keep tears from flowing—"more than I can give."

His breath hitched. "You're more than I deserve. You've been honest with me. I know what I'm getting myself into."

"Do you?" she asked honestly because she wasn't so sure he did.

"I do." His tone was firm.

She wanted to believe him, but the way he'd kissed her…

Madeleine glanced at the seat. Only a sliver of black leather remained between his pinky finger and hers.

Her mouth went dry. She didn't know if she'd moved her hand or if he had. Worse, she wanted to bridge the space left.

"You lost the man you loved, the one you chose to marry. I can never replace him. I wouldn't want to try." His hand covered hers, the touch of his warm skin bringing an odd mixture of relief and regret. "But we can have a family, rule the kingdom, and improve the lives of people in Gaullia and on the island."

The lump in her throat grew. Madeleine stared at their hands. If she spread her fingers, his might fall between hers and she could hold his hand. But inhaling was difficult enough. She…couldn't. Not when he was talking about having a family with her. "If I'm freaking out this much over a kiss, I'm not sure I'm ready for…more."

"So we wait. Postpone the honeymoon. No big deal."

Some of her unease disappeared. She raised her gaze to meet his. "Really?"

It was his turn to nod. "A marriage takes two people working together to be successful. I won't push you into something you're not ready for."

She half laughed. "You've been called selfish and self-centered, but you're nothing like that."

A sheepish grin formed. "I was, and I still can be. But when I'm with you, I no longer see myself. My focus is you. Us. I want to do better. Be better." He shook his head. "I'm probably not making any sense."

Madeleine leaned toward him. "I understand."

"That makes one of us."

She smiled. "I just…"

"Need more time." The compassion in his eyes matched his voice.

She nodded. "I'll try not to freak out on our wedding day."

"Perhaps we should pretend to kiss," he suggested. "No one will be the wiser."

His thoughtfulness tugged on her heart. If only they could pretend, but… "Given the wedding will be televised, an actual kiss, or rather a peck, might be safer, or someone might make an enlarged, slow-motion clip of us not kissing."

"A peck it is."

Silence filled the limousine. Once again, the comfortableness of the quiet struck her. He left his hand covering hers. His simple gesture soothed her.

The lump in her throat shrank. Tears no longer pricked her eyes. Tension unexpectedly released.

Madeleine exhaled. She hoped this was the only crisis that erupted before the wedding. But if another did, Enrique would help her get through it. "Thank you."

He smiled warmly. "You're welcome, my princess."

At the palace, Enrique escorted Madeleine to her room. He wanted to hold her hand, to touch her the way he had in the limousine, to prove to himself he hadn't made a mistake by kissing her and messed up the wedding.

And his future.

Her face wasn't as flushed, but the wariness in her eyes remained. That worried him. She claimed he'd done nothing wrong, but he didn't believe her. Making mistakes was part of his DNA.

"Rest." He opened her bedroom door before motioning her inside. "I will ask Mrs. Hobbs to work her magic and cancel your remaining appearances for today."

The corners of Madeleine's mouth edged up. "Mrs. Hobbs isn't a magician with a wand."

Not much of a smile, but better than a frown.

Or tears.

She'd been on the verge of crying when he'd slid onto the seat next to her in the limousine. "No, but if Mrs. Hobbs is anything like our Ortiz, she has a few tricks she keeps secret that she calls upon as necessary."

Madeleine nodded. "What are you going to do?"

Whatever I need to do so you can relax and unwind.

"I'll complete my itinerary." Enrique wanted to stay to make sure she was okay, but he couldn't push her. Instead, he would offer his services to Mrs. Hobbs and fulfill any of Madeleine's obligations that couldn't be canceled or rescheduled.

Her eyes clouded.

Enrique recognized the fear on her face. He'd seen the same look after they'd kissed.

His heart hammered, a mixture of wanting to protect her and an apprehension she would back out of their marriage contract. Not to mention a longing to kiss her again.

Her lips parted. "I—"

He placed his finger against her mouth. "You're stressed. You appear worn out. Don't push yourself. We can talk when I return."

By then, Enrique hoped he was ready to hear what she had to say.

For better or for worse.

Madeleine nodded. "You're right."

Enrique released the breath he'd been holding. He bowed slightly. "Until later."

Much later, he realized.

Following a brief chat with Mrs. Hobbs, Enrique was in the limo again. He missed having Madeleine seated next to him, their hands touching, but she needed to rest.

His first stop was a grand opening of a library. He cut the ribbon, posed for photographs, and shook hands. Next was an appearance at a farmers market to sample fresh fruits and vegetables with more photographers present. Finally, he arrived for a press conference with journalism students at the lone university in the country. He and Madeleine were supposed to attend together, but he gave her regrets for not being there.

Standing behind a podium, he stared at the auditorium full of eager college students. A professor was acting as moderator so Enrique could focus on the questions.

A young woman with thick glasses stood. "What are your feelings on arranged marriages given it's the twenty-first century and women aren't chattel?"

This question would please Jules. "I want to talk about the second part of your question first. La Isla de la Aurora and many other countries across the globe believe and support equal rights for women. A few don't share that view, but some are trying to modernize their laws. No one can change the past, but we can make a difference now. And are."

Students scribbled on notebooks and typed on

their phones and tablets.

"Implying Her Royal Highness Madeleine-Victoria is chattel because she's agreed to a marriage that benefits her country and mine is wrong. For centuries, arranged marriages between royals have occurred. Less nowadays, but our match wasn't forced upon either of us." Granted, Enrique would pay the price if he'd said no, but the choice had been his. Just as Madeleine had chosen him. "It doesn't matter whether you're a student or a crown prince, dating is hard these days. Swiping right or left? Imagine using a dating app when the first thing your bodyguard wants to do is run a background check on the person before you contact them."

The audience laughed. More jotted notes.

"I'm thrilled to match with Madeleine and excited for our wedding." He hoped she felt the same way. "The princess is a wonderful, intelligent, eloquent woman who will also be a fantastic wife, mother, and queen."

A young man with short blond hair and intense brown eyes sprang to his feet. "Did you know Crown Prince Louie?"

The question didn't surprise Enrique. The crown prince had been beloved and well-known everywhere, but especially in Gaullia because of the royal romance and engagement. "Prince Louie and I attended the same boarding school. He was younger than me, so we'd met a few times but weren't in the same social circle. He was friendly and outgoing. He would have been an excellent ruler. His death was a terrible loss."

"He was the princess's first fiancé," the same student continued as if her past had been kept from Enrique. "How would you compare yourself to him?"

"I…" Enrique remembered what Alejandro and Jules had told him—think before he spoke. The question wasn't one Enrique had expected to answer, but he understood the curiosity. Physically the two men were opposites, from their coloring to their builds, but that wasn't what the student meant.

"I can't compare myself to Louie," Enrique said finally, even though his answer would likely disappoint the budding journalists. "We are from two different countries and types of governments. He died at a young age, before showing what he could do as a ruler. We may share the same title but nothing else."

A young woman with her hair pulled back stood. "What about Princess Madeleine?"

Sweat beaded at Enrique's neck. "Louie was engaged to her for longer."

The crowd laughed, but that didn't relax his tight muscles.

People found royals entertaining. That came with the title, but discussing his personal life made him uncomfortable. Madeleine's love for Louie wasn't a secret. Enrique would give her the time she needed, but these questions fueled his insecurities about her backing out of the wedding.

Time to take charge before this press conference ended up turning into a daytime talk show complete with soundbites about chattel and a dead fiancé.

He surveyed the crowd. The young, bright-eyed faces had their lives ahead of them. A part of him wished he could be in his early twenties again and start over, knowing what he knew now.

"Any questions about Gaullia and La Isla de la Aurora?" he asked.

Thirty minutes later, Enrique was in the limousine on his way to the next appearance. Tired and thirsty, he chugged a bottle of water. Overall, he thought the press conference went well. He could speak about economics and politics for hours. Anything else made him uncomfortable. Only time would tell if he'd inserted his foot into his mouth again, but he'd tried.

He leaned against the leather seat before pulling out his cell phone and calling Alejandro.

His brother picked up on the second ring. "Did you kiss her yet?"

"That's how you greet me?" Enrique asked.

"Answer the question, bro."

Unsure how much he wanted to share, he combed his hair with his fingers. "We kissed during our wedding rehearsal, to practice."

"Not what I had in mind."

"Sorry to disappoint." He, however, hadn't been disappointed. The kiss had been perfect, but he wished she hadn't blamed herself for kissing him back.

The question from the press conference slammed into him.

Heat rushed through his veins, forcing him to adjust a vent so air flowed onto him before he overheated. He'd assumed her reaction had been because of grief, but had she been comparing his kiss to Louie's?

Enrique's left arm itched.

"I shouldn't complain," Alejandro said. "You put your lips against hers. Was there a spark?"

Enough to set off an explosion. But sharing that with his brother or anyone didn't feel right. "There's chemistry."

Alejandro laughed. "Have fun on the honeymoon."

"We may postpone that."

"Why?" His brother sounded perplexed. Of course he did, given he was head over heels in love with Jules.

"Madeleine and I are strangers," Enrique explained. "I'm trying to make this easier on her. She needs more time to get to know me before we, er—"

"Make babies," Alejandro teased.

"Right." Enrique's cheeks burned.

His brother laughed. "What are you doing now?"

"I'm in a limousine on my way to make an appearance somewhere. I'm filling in for Madeleine. After the rehearsal, she needed a break."

"Your kiss got to her." Alejandro snickered. "Way to go, bro."

Unfortunately, her reaction was nothing to cheer about. But Enrique didn't want to share that, either. "It was a long morning."

"Well, everything is looking up. That's great."

"The kiss wasn't a big deal." Okay, it had been to him, but he needed to downplay that, given the circumstances.

"I'm not talking about the kiss," Alejandro said to Enrique's surprise. "You've spent your life being selfish and self-centered."

The words stung, but Enrique couldn't deny them. "True."

"But you've changed. Two years ago, you would have never put Madeleine first. Jules will be proud. I am."

The words sank in. Putting Madeleine's wants and needs first wasn't a conscious effort. He'd just done it. "Thanks, but I'm grateful for her agreeing to marry me."

"This match will be good for you."

"Yes." He wanted to be a man worthy of her. That meant doing and being his best, in every situation. Even the uncomfortable ones. "It will be."

The limousine pulled to a curb.

"Duty calls," Enrique said. "I have to go."

"Keep kissing her."

He would if he could. "Say hi to Jules for me. Niko and Izzy, too."

By the time Enrique had tucked his phone into his

pocket, the limousine's door was open. Captain Mendoza stood next to the driver. "Your next stop, sir."

Enrique stared at the building in front of him—a hospital. His jaw clenched. His heart raced. Black spots appeared.

A man—Enrique squinted to see him clearly—walked toward him. "Welcome, Your Highness. We're sorry Princess Madeleine couldn't be here today, but the patients are excited for your visit."

Enrique took a step back.

"I'll be your escort," the man continued. "Are you ready?"

No. Enrique swallowed.

You must do this.

As his heartbeat roared in his ears, he stuck his hand into his jacket pocket and wrapped his fingers around the bottle of hand sanitizer from Reggie. "Yes, I'm ready."

This might turn into a nightmare, but he had to try.

For Madeleine, he would.

Chapter Thirteen

Dinner wasn't for another hour, but Madeleine didn't want to wait to see Enrique. A nap and a bubble bath had helped her relax.

She couldn't change how she'd responded to his kiss or the guilt for enjoying it so much, but beating herself up over it would solve nothing. All she could do was move forward, however clumsily. Or at least try, given it was something she'd struggled to do for five years.

Standing at his bedroom door, she knocked.

Silence greeted her.

Maybe he'd been delayed returning to the castle or had a conference call or wore earbuds so he hadn't heard her.

Madeleine knocked again. Wiggled her toes.

No answer.

She stepped to her left, leaned her back against the wall, and tilted her head to stare at the ceiling. Eyes closed, she sighed.

She wanted to see him. To apologize. Again.

If she'd handled the kiss better, taking the afternoon off wouldn't have been necessary. Her naptime dream wouldn't have featured both Louie and Enrique, in a tangled romantic web. She wouldn't be facing a different kind of panic.

About the upcoming wedding.

About kissing Enrique again.

About what being husband and wife would entail once they arrived on La Isla de la Aurora.

Madeleine opened her eyes. She fought the urge to wipe her palms against her dress. She shouldn't be nervous. Enrique hadn't appeared upset earlier. He'd been concerned, accepting, and understanding. He would give her time to get used to him and their relationship. That was more than she could hope for under the circumstances.

Which was why she wanted him to know, despite freaking out today, she was committed to marrying him on Saturday.

"Are you looking for Prince Enrique, ma'am?"

Mrs. Hobbs asked, approaching from the king's suite.

"I am. Have you seen him?"

"Prince Enrique is in the garden, ma'am."

Tension uncoiled. Madeleine straightened, eager to see him.

"Poor man." Mrs. Hobbs shook her head. "I fear the final stop was too much for him. A formal dinner with the king and queen is the last thing he needs. I offered to send his regrets to your parents and have a tray brought to his room."

Madeleine couldn't remember his itinerary. "Where did he go last?"

"The hospital."

Her jaw dropped. Muscles bunched. "That's impossible. He wasn't supposed to make another visit there."

"It wasn't on his schedule, but yours." Mrs. Hobbs's gaze softened. "He fulfilled both itineraries today."

Oh, Enrique. A weight pressed against Madeleine's chest. While she rested, he'd been doing his duty and hers. Guilt burned deep.

He must be upset and seeking solace in the garden. She'd done something similar.

After her nap and bath, she'd asked Lilia to bring up an embroidery project. Madeleine had thrown herself into creating leaves using a padded satin stitch. Focusing on the up and down of the needle, keeping the stitches parallel and next to each other melted away her stress. Not all of it, but she wasn't as on edge as earlier. She hoped Enrique found similar relief.

"Is there anything else you need, ma'am?" Mrs. Hobbs asked.

Enrique. But Madeleine would find him herself. Forget wanting dinner tonight. She'd lost her appetite. "No, thank you, but please prepare two meal trays and pass on my regrets to my parents."

Mrs. Hobbs studied her. "Are you ill, ma'am?"

"No," Madeleine answered quickly. She didn't want anyone to worry about her. They'd done enough of that. "I need a break."

"Not a problem, ma'am." Mrs. Hobbs tapped on her phone. "The good news is you'll be able to relax soon."

Mrs. Hobbs meant after the wedding.

True, but…

Madeleine had a feeling marriage would only increase her stress level. Nodding, she bit the inside of her cheek.

"A tray will be delivered promptly at seven," Mrs. Hobbs said. "Enjoy the rest of your day, ma'am."

"Thank you."

As Mrs. Hobbs walked away, Madeleine headed out the exit and to the garden. The few wisps of clouds didn't block the sun's strong rays. But she'd take the heat over rain. Her sleeveless dress and sandals would keep her from getting too hot.

A glimpse at the top of the fountain sent a stabbing pain shooting through her stomach. Nothing she hadn't experienced before, but her grief was stronger today, sharp-edged rather than the usual dull ache.

Because of the kiss.

Enrique's kiss.

She touched her mouth.

Her lips no longer throbbed, but the memory remained, one that was erasing past kisses she wanted to remember and cherish forever.

"I miss you, Louie. I don't want to replace you. Not that I could," she whispered to her love. "But I need to marry Enrique. Gaullia is counting on me, yet I'm afraid to leave this place where you and I fell in love. To have a family with another man. To…live."

A bird landed on the fountain. Only for a moment before flying away.

"Please help me, Louie." Her voice cracked. "You always knew what to do. You were the strong one. I need your strength now."

Madeleine didn't expect an answer or a sign, but speaking the words instead of keeping them inside her helped.

Her gaze lingered on the fountain before she continued farther into the garden to find Enrique. On the far side, she saw him from behind, standing in front of a rose bush. He focused on the flowers, oblivious to everything around him, including her.

She did a double take.

Blinked.

Froze in place, her breath catching in her throat.

No suit.

His blue shorts reminded her of the lightweight nylon kind Karl wore when he worked out, but her brother never looked like…that. A fitted white T-shirt showed Enrique's wide shoulders and toned muscles. Not huge ones like a bodybuilder. Perfect-sized ones.

His skin glistened from a light sheen of sweat. Physical awareness buzzed through her.

She gulped.

Not what she needed right now.

Running away would be the smart thing to do after the kissing fiasco earlier, but she wanted to talk to him for that exact reason and hear about his hospital visit. Putting off the discussion wouldn't solve anything.

She watched him reach forward. A clip sounded, and then he dropped something into the bucket at his feet. He did it again and again.

The fabric at the back of his neck darkened as if damp—sweat.

Madeleine enjoyed seeing him like this, but she was overheating from the inside out. Something she couldn't blame on the warm temperature.

Even though she wanted to keep enjoying the view, she couldn't. Well, shouldn't. She cleared her dry throat to let him know she was here.

He glanced over his shoulder. His eyes widened, and his mouth fell open, but then he pressed his lips together.

She forced a smile. "Gardening?"

Enrique faced her. Wariness was written on his face. He held pruning shears in his right hand. In his left was a wilted rose, which he then dropped into the bucket. "Deadheading with the palace gardener's permission."

"The roses look prettier now."

"They do, and deadheading keeps a garden looking nice, but removing the dead flowers has another purpose. A more practical one by helping a plant, or in this case a rose bush, make more blossoms rather than seeds." He gripped the clippers until his knuckles went white. "I doubt you came out here for a gardening lesson."

"No, but I'd like to learn more."

Enrique stepped back, his shoulders crumpling. "You would?"

She nodded, not understanding why he sounded so surprised. "Yes, but not now. Mrs. Hobbs mentioned you visited the hospital. Are you okay?"

His jaw tightened. "I…survived."

His words and quiet voice didn't tell Madeleine much, especially given how badly the last time turned out. "I imagine going there was difficult."

With a nod, he turned, snipped a wilted, brown

blossom and then threw it into the bucket.

His silence worried her. She didn't want him to relive the visit, but she had to know what kind of damage control would be necessary. "How did it go?"

He shifted his weight between his feet. "Better than the last time."

She moved closer to him. "Great."

Enrique shrugged. "The hospital administrator offered me a pair of gloves to wear. Between those and Reggie's hand sanitizer, I managed. No press conference will be required."

Thank goodness. Maybe now her heart rate would slow. "I'm so happy to hear that."

His brows pulled in, giving him a pensive expression. "A hospital visit shouldn't be an issue. I hate that it is."

"Today it wasn't." She touched his forearm, his skin warm and damp. "You let nothing get in the way of your visit. That's big progress."

Gratitude reflected in his gaze. "Thanks. I didn't want to disappoint you."

Again was implied.

"You didn't." She was still touching him and pulled back her arm. "I'm proud of you."

The corners of his mouth curved.

"I wish I could do the same thing," she admitted. "I—"

"You," Enrique said at the same time. He blew out

a breath. "Go ahead. You came out here for a reason."

"I…" She bit her lip. "Can we talk?"

"Of course. The flowers can wait." Enrique placed the shears next to the bucket before brushing his hands together. "Let's sit in the shade. It's hot out."

You're the hot one.

She shook the thought from her head. She must still be rattled from the kiss or seeing him dressed differently.

He led her to a bench shaded by a large evergreen tree.

Madeleine sat. He did, too, taking a spot as far away from her as possible. She needed time. Maybe he was also giving her space.

The lines around his mouth deepened as did the creases on his forehead. His pale skin tone suggested the gardening hadn't relaxed him. He wiped his hands on his shorts. "What do you want to talk about?"

Her heart pounded. "I meant what I said about wishing I could do the same thing you did today. You've been so understanding about my…grief and needing time. I only wish I knew how long that will take."

"You can't rush through your grief. There is no timetable."

"Not everyone thinks that. Many keep telling me to move on."

"I will never do that." He spoke firmly without an

ounce of hesitation or doubt.

"I know." Madeleine wasn't sure how, but she did. "That's why I wanted to talk to you. Today didn't turn out as either of us planned. I have no idea what the next few days will hold or our wedding, but I'll do my best. I won't let you down."

His intense gaze narrowed. "You still want to marry me?"

"Of course."

Sagging against the bench, he blinked once. Twice. "I thought you were calling it off."

"No, I would never do that. I'm committed to our wedding contract. To our marriage." The words rushed out, one on top of another. She forced herself to slow down. "But I wouldn't blame you if you wanted out given my…issues."

"I don't. I…" Enrique rubbed his hand over his face. He left a smudge of dirt on his cheek. "Sorry. I was certain you were sending me away."

"You're not going anywhere except to the cathedral on Saturday."

His mouth slanted. "What about the cake-tasting and final wedding rehearsal?"

So literal. She laughed. "We'll go to those places as well."

She raised her hand to clean his face.

When she touched him, he stiffened.

"You have dirt on your cheek." With her thumb,

she removed it. "All gone."

He said nothing.

She lowered her hand. "I hope you know I don't want you leaving Gaullia without me."

Her country needed this marriage, but a part of her appeared to want it, too.

As Enrique stared up at the sky, his profile showed off his chiseled cheekbones. All the parts of his face fit so perfectly. Gorgeous. Strong.

"Hearing you say that makes me so happy." He inhaled deeply. "Thank you."

His deep, warm voice washed over her like a caress. She tingled all over. She opened her mouth, but no words came out so she smiled.

His face brightened, his smile crinkling the corners of his eyes.

A good thing she was sitting or her knees might have wobbled. Finding her husband attractive shouldn't be a problem. But these feelings were uncomfortable. She didn't like having them.

Not about someone other than Louie.

"Want to help me with the flowers?" Enrique asked.

The hopeful gleam in his eyes warmed her heart. He wasn't what she'd expected. Despite his flaws and faults, Enrique was kindhearted. She couldn't ask for more than that. "Yes, I would enjoy working in the garden with you. But I'll need instructions. Other than weeding, I have no idea what I'm doing."

Enrique reached out his hand but then placed his arm at his side. He smiled at her. "Consider it your first lesson in gardening, my princess."

Chapter Fourteen

The time Enrique spent with Madeleine in the garden talking and deadheading roses brought a sense of peace. His fears of being told to leave the castle—and the country—hadn't disappeared completely. Nightmares about Alejandro's coronation woke Enrique in the early hours each morning. But hope the wedding would occur was winning the battle against his doubts.

The best part?

He wasn't on his own.

Yes, he had his father and brother on the island.

Jules and the staff, too. But beyond the walls of the palace, Enrique's circle of friends was small. Okay, miniscule. Dating wasn't the only thing he found difficult. Making and keeping friends was, too.

The few friends who remained after university were there because he would one day be king. Without his title, they would never speak with him again. Enrique knew they were attending the wedding to be seen at the event, not to witness his big day.

Madeleine, however, was different. She understood him—everything from his dislike of the media to his obsession with gardening. Their friendship grew stronger each day. They were partners. That showed during meals, walks, or passing each other in the hallway. That boded well for their marriage.

All they had to do was survive the interviews, ribbon-cutting ceremonies, visits, and press conferences. And of course, the wedding on Saturday.

Only days away.

Which was why they were being driven in a limousine to the cake tasting.

She sat next to him, their shoulders touching. He wasn't used to that. Normally, he preferred keeping his distance, but not with Madeleine.

Today, she wore her hair loose, falling past her shoulders in soft curls. The dark brown strands contrasted against her lavender jacket. Her nude pumps accentuated her legs, making them appear longer.

Madeleine checked the time on her phone. "Today should be fun."

"If not fun, then tasty."

She angled toward him, bringing her legs closer to him. "I hope there's more than one chocolate cake to try. I don't mind the other flavors, but—"

"Chocolate is your favorite."

She nodded. "If daisies are part of the wedding, then chocolate cake should be, too."

"Do we get more than one flavor?" he asked.

She scrunched her nose. "I have no idea. My mother had a cake in mind, so she coordinated with the wedding planner."

"Then we'll ask the baker."

A crowd gathered in the street. The limousine couldn't get close to the curb, so it stopped in the middle of the road.

"Stay in the car, Your Highnesses," the driver said to them. "A security team will see you safely inside."

Enrique peered out the window. Cameramen and reporters jockeyed for position in front of a quaint bakery. He didn't know how all of them would fit inside. Nor did he want them there. Not that he had a choice. He flexed his fingers.

Madeleine patted his hand. "The press is staying outside. They'll be able to film through the front door and windows, but none will be in the bakery."

Her words didn't reassure him, but he appreciated the effort.

A back door opened. Captain Mendoza leaned inside. "The security team has formed a passageway into the bakery. Keep moving until you are inside. Do not stop to answer any questions or pose for photos."

"Sounds easy enough," Enrique quipped.

Madeleine nodded. "Nothing I haven't done before."

No, but he hated this part. Thinking about people reaching out to touch him, either on purpose or by accident, made him shudder.

"It'll be fine, sir," Captain Mendoza said. "Let's go."

Madeleine slid out of the limousine first. Her bodyguard had her moving before Enrique could get out. As he found himself shuffled inside, people shouted questions.

"Where are you honeymooning?"

"Is the princess expecting?"

"Will you miss Gaullia?"

"Does the crown prince have OCD?"

Enrique tuned out the voices, letting them blur into a sound he called gray noise. Someone touched his shoulder.

He tensed.

It was a palace guard. "We're almost inside, sir."

"I've got him." Captain Mendoza pushed the guard's hand off Enrique. "Keep moving, sir."

Seconds later, Enrique entered the bakery to find a line of smiling staff members dressed in white with gold aprons and their heads covered in hairnets.

A middle-aged man with a receding hairline bowed. "Thank you for gracing us with your presence, Your Highness. I am Uwe van Meter. This is my bakery."

Enrique shook the man's hand. "Thank you for hosting our tasting and baking our wedding cake."

Uwe beamed. "I'm honored to be a participant in the royal nuptials. Please join the princess at the tasting table."

A linen tablecloth covered a rectangular table where Madeleine sat. The only problem? She faced the windows so the press had a clear shot of them.

Enrique's stomach knotted. No problem. He'd been told there would be media coverage. This was part of being royal, but he wished they were doing this alone, just the two of them at the bakery.

He sat in the chair next to Madeleine. In front of each of them was a piece of paper with ten numbers on it and a pen.

Uwe stood to the side as if not to block any camera shots. "I was told neither of you have any food allergies."

"I don't," Madeleine said.

"Neither do I," Enrique added.

"Excellent." Uwe motioned to each of their place settings. "You will taste ten cakes tonight. Please write down your thoughts. At the end, your notes will decide what flavors you want. The queen has offered her input already."

Madeleine half laughed. "Of course she has."

Enrique chuckled, placing his napkin on his lap. If not for the media interest in the royal wedding, the queen would have made the decision herself and not had them do a tasting.

The baker clapped. The sharp sound traveled through the shop.

An employee carried a small white frosted cake to the table. A quarter of it was missing, but the gap showed three layers of white cake with white filling. Another staff member set a plate containing a slice in front of Madeleine and then him.

Madeleine examined the cake. "This one is very…bridal."

Enrique translated that to mean not chocolate.

Outside, someone tapped on the window.

Enrique glanced up, only to see cameras pointed in his direction. Uncomfortable, he shifted in his seat. His appetite for cake disappeared.

Pull yourself together.

He breathed in and out. That didn't help. Maybe if he tried again…

Madeleine reached under the table and squeezed his hand.

They shared a glance, one that calmed him.

"I have an idea. The wedding cake has many traditions associated with it." She filled her fork with a bite of cake. "Slicing the cake is the first task a married couple does together, symbolizing their partnership in the years ahead. Feeding each other bites of the first slice symbolizes a couple's commitment to provide for each other. So let's practice."

He stared at his plate. "The cake's already sliced."

Mischief twinkled in her eyes. "That's why we're going to practice feeding each other."

Temptation flared, followed by a burst of anticipation. Then, common sense set in. "I…"

She brought the fork to his mouth before he could say anything else. "Taste it."

Even though he knew she was doing this for the press outside the window, a part of him wished they were a bride and groom who would be declaring their love in the cathedral on Saturday.

Enrique gripped the sides of his chair. She fed him the cake and then lowered the fork.

Sugary sweetness from the icing exploded in his mouth. The cake itself was light and moist with a hint of almond. The two created a perfect combination. Not as lackluster as he thought a plain white cake might be. "Delicious."

Uwe's chest puffed out. "This is a traditional wedding cake flavor. I've created my own special recipe. Be sure to jot down your opinion of it."

Enrique did before picking up a forkful of cake. He angled toward Madeleine. "Your turn."

He tried to keep his hand steady but managed to smear icing above her lip before putting the fork into her mouth. "Sorry."

She chewed and then swallowed. "It's not as easy as it looks. By the ninth or tenth cake, we'll know what we're doing."

He used a napkin to gently wipe off the icing. If they were a real couple, he could have licked it off.

The thought sent his temperature up.

Unless it was nerves. Likely nerves.

She wrote something next to the number one on her paper.

The plates, forks, and cake were removed from the table. New place settings were brought out followed by another cake. As the process continued—so did feeding each other.

By the fifth cake, the tension was gone. Laughter ensued when Madeleine kept waiting to see if the next one they'd taste would be chocolate. When it wasn't, she would deflate for a second but perk up with the arrival of the next cake to taste.

Someone knocked on the window. They heard the refrains of "Kiss, kiss, kiss."

That was odd since no one had asked for public displays of affection before today.

"Ignore them," Madeleine whispered.

Enrique would try, but after feeding her, a kiss didn't seem like such a stretch.

Except there wasn't supposed to be more kissing.

Only a peck at the ceremony.

"We have two more to go," Uwe announced.

A young man carried out plates with slices from a

layered chocolate cake with white icing.

"Finally," Madeleine mumbled.

He tried not to laugh. "It's the one you've been waiting for."

"Not quite," she replied in a low voice. "The icing isn't chocolate."

"This isn't the last one," he reminded her.

That earned him a wide smile.

If only he could elicit the same response chocolate did.

They fed each other again. Each time was easier, so the practice was helping.

As he wrote his opinion, Madeleine starred this one. She hadn't done that with any of the others.

The next cake brought out was chocolate with fudge icing.

Madeleine sucked in a breath.

He leaned closer to her. "Your wish has come true, my princess."

She wet her lips. "Can we pick this one and be finished?"

"Don't you want a taste?" he asked because this was her favorite.

"I suppose we shouldn't let the slices go to waste."

"I applaud your sense of duty," he teased. "You can taste the first bite."

"No, you. I know I'll love it."

"Thank you, my princess."

Smiling, she fed him the cake.

His lips had only closed on the fork when the chocolate filled his mouth. Deep, rich. He wanted another taste. Something he hadn't wanted with the other flavors. He made a note and then placed the pen on the table.

It was her turn. Anticipation gleamed in her eyes.

As soon as he removed his fork from her mouth, her eyes closed. A dreamy expression formed on her face.

A fluttery sensation filled his stomach. Was that what people meant by feeling butterflies?

"Mmmmm." She opened her eyes.

Her reaction told him this flavor would be a top choice, if not number one. She wrote on her paper and then drew a heart.

"Are you finished?" Uwe asked.

"We are," Enrique said.

Uwe picked up their sheets. "I will see which are your top flavors."

With that, the baker disappeared into the back. The plates, forks, and cake were picked up by staff members.

"They would take the one I wanted more of," she joked. "The last one was perfection."

"Your favorite."

She nodded. "I enjoy chocolate."

"You love chocolate," he corrected.

"I do." Madeleine studied him. "You know my favorite, but what's yours? Not the cake we tasted, but dessert.”

“Mantecados,” he said without hesitation. “They are cookies made at Christmastime. They aren’t chocolate but soft and melt in your mouth.”

“*Manteca* means butter.”

He hadn’t known she spoke Spanish. “Or lard. That’s where the name came from.”

“I look forward to tasting one during the holidays.”

“Eating only one is impossible.”

“That’s because they are your favorites, but perhaps they’ll become mine, too.”

Their gazes met. A connection seemed to flow between them.

Another round of “kiss, kiss, kiss” came from outside.

“They aren’t giving up,” she said.

“Ignore them.” Things were going well. He didn’t want anything, including the reporters, to ruin the outing. “They only want photos to use as click-bait.”

“Yes, but…” Her mouth slanted.

“What?”

She leaned closer to him, her warm breath against his neck. “We could practice a peck.”

A peck, not a kiss.

That was more than he imagined her wanting. “Are you sure?”

She nodded.

That was the only invitation he needed.

Enrique brought his mouth to hers. The moment

their lips touched, the meaning of *perfection* changed. Forget chocolate, her kiss was the new definition.

Sweet. The combination of the icings, cakes, and her warmth gave him a taste of heaven on earth. He would never be able to get enough of it.

Of her.

His lips moved over hers, and she increased the pressure as if wanting more.

Uh-oh. This wasn't a peck but a full-blown kiss.

Exactly what his lips wanted, but not what they'd agreed upon.

He drew back.

She stared at him, her pupils dilated and her breathing rushed.

Would she freak out again?

He waited, unsure what to say or do, afraid to make another mistake.

Madeleine's lip curved into a closed-mouth smile. "I'm sure we gave them some clickable photos."

He released the breath he'd been holding before focusing on the crowd at the window. "They appear pleased."

"Yes."

Was she? He didn't dare ask.

A few people waved. Some gave them the thumbs-up.

She waved so he did, too.

"This has been a fun outing," she said.

He wouldn't forget her feeding him bites of cake,

the feel of her lips against his, and the taste of her kiss. Even with the press watching, he enjoyed being with her. Seeing her happy pleased him.

Something unfurled inside him.

He cared about Madeleine in a way he'd never cared about anyone else.

Because you're marrying her.

That had to be it. Except…

He hadn't felt this way about Jules. Not even close.

Enrique had planned their wedding to be what he wanted. Never consulting Jules or even considering her wishes. He didn't know if a groomzilla existed, but he'd been one. With Madeleine, none of this was about him. He wanted their wedding to make her happy—to give her what she desired. And not only because marrying her meant he'd be king.

What did it mean?

He had no idea, but he hoped he found out sooner rather than later. With the wedding so close, he couldn't afford to mess up.

Again.

Chapter Fiftteen

Two days before the wedding, Madeleine played a mannequin, standing on a platform in the ballroom while attendants buttoned her wedding gown. Her mother and the designer, a talented woman named Delia, stood nearby supervising.

Lilia covered her mouth with her hand. "Oh, ma'am. It's beautiful. I knew the gown would be lovely on you, but you're the quintessential princess bride."

Lilia wore her heart on her sleeve. Any show of emotion was genuine, unfiltered by the training Mrs. Hobbs attempted to instill in the staff. But that was one reason Madeleine loved Lilia and wished she could go to the island with her. She'd been offered the position, but her husband's job and their families were in Gaullia, so she'd said no. Which Madeleine understood, but she would miss her.

"Thanks. The tiara helps with that."

The women laughed.

What Madeleine said wasn't that funny, but it was true. A tiara, designer clothes, talented staff—stylist, hair designer, maid—could make any woman look like a princess.

Lilia's eyes twinkled with excitement. "The dress, too."

It had been hanging in Madeleine's room until this morning. Each glance had brought a sense of dread. She'd tried on the gown twice before, but she hadn't wanted to try it on again. Not when the idea of the upcoming wedding to a total stranger had been a living nightmare. Which was why she'd put off the final fitting until today.

But now…

Wearing yards of white fabric no longer panicked her. Anticipation had replaced that. To be honest, she couldn't wait to face the mirrors behind her. Not because she doubted the compliments, but because there was a more important reason.

"Do you think Enrique will like it?" she asked.

Her mother beamed. She walked in a semicircle as if to view the front of the gown from every direction.

"He will love it. The dress is perfect for you."

Madeleine's stomach was all fluttery. She wanted to look her best for Enrique on Saturday. She wanted him to be proud to call her his bride. He was far from perfect, but he was trying his best. He didn't know by marrying her he would be Gaullia's hero, but she did. "Guess I'll find out soon enough."

Enrique wouldn't get a glimpse of her in the gown until she entered the cathedral. That, however, seemed too far away. She wished the wedding were today or tomorrow.

That surprised Madeleine. At times, the thought of leaving Gaullia still reduced her to tears. Yet she had to move to be with Enrique. And she wanted that. He'd become important to her. Not only as her future husband but also as her friend—a partner in crime in the lead-up to the royal wedding.

Upon meeting him, she couldn't stand him, but he'd grown on Madeleine in unexpected ways. She was no longer all alone. When she was with Enrique, smiles and laughter came easier. He also didn't pressure her in ways her family did. Not once had he told her what she *should* do or treated her like a child who couldn't decide for herself.

His acceptance meant the world to her, gave her hope, filled her with affection for him. He was a kind man. He would be a good husband.

"Enrique will have no complaints." Her mother cupped her chin. "You make an exquisite bride."

Madeleine glanced at the intricate applique on the skirt. "Delia deserves the praise for her design and the craftmanship."

Delia's face brightened. "Designing for you is easy, ma'am. Anything will look gorgeous while you're wearing it."

Madeleine's face heated. "Thank you."

"You look like a queen." An odd expression formed on her mother's face. "It's something I've imagined you being, but now I see it."

The emotion in her mother's voice surprised Madeleine. "I still feel like a princess."

"That will change," the queen said.

Madeleine shrugged. She needed to get used to being Enrique's wife before she thought about anything else.

Delia rubbed her hands together. "Are you ready to see yourself?"

Excitement shot through Madeleine. "Yes, please."

The designer motioned for her to turn.

As she did, attendants held the gown's long train, moving as Madeleine did.

Facing the mirror, her heart thudded. She'd worn tiaras before. She'd tried on this dress twice. But today...

Her breathing sped up. Tears pricked her eyes. "I'm a bride."

Logically, she knew that, given her wedding was two days away. But seeing her reflection this time made it real. She felt different—more alive.

I'm getting married.

"Yes, you are, dear." Her mother laughed.

Oops. Madeleine hadn't realized she'd spoken aloud.

Delia surveyed the gown. "Feels more real now, doesn't it?"

Not trusting her voice, Madeleine nodded.

Very real.

That frightened her.

She feared like the last time she'd been engaged, the wedding wouldn't happen. Yet she couldn't deny at the same time she was hopeful.

So, so hopeful.

For Gaullia.

For Enrique.

For herself.

Even though apathy had kept her from being an active participant in the design process, Madeleine had zero complaints over how her wedding gown turned out. The dress was exactly what she would have chosen for herself.

"A thank you isn't enough, Delia."

She imagined floating along the aisle, a vision in white, toward Enrique, the organ music bellowing throughout the cathedral. All heads would turn her way, but she would be focused on her future husband, smiling and eager, waiting for her.

A sigh welled inside Madeleine.

"She appears to like the dress," her mother stated matter-of-factly.

"More like loves it, ma'am," Lilia said, amusement in her voice.

"I do." Madeleine hadn't meant to say the words so forcefully, but she had. Giggles and laughter filled the room. But this dress was almost magical. She had stopped believing in happy endings, but she would settle for being happy.

Perhaps marrying Enrique could save her and her country.

On the day before the royal wedding, Madeleine attended the final rehearsal, which went smoother than the first one. Although, the page boys and flower girls ran wild in the vestibule, despite their nannies' orders. The children fed off each other, seeing who could act up the most. Still, their smiling, giggling faces warmed Madeleine's heart.

No tears today.

At least not from her.

A headstrong five-year-old named Penelope wailed like a banshee because she wanted to walk with the page boys and hold their hands. Chaos ensued, until the wedding planner pulled out pieces of candy from her pocket. The tears stopped long enough for the rehearsal to continue.

When the time came for a kiss, the rapid touch of Enrique's lips against Madeleine's could barely be called a peck. Good practice for tomorrow, but the kiss itself bothered her. Weird, since a peck was what they'd agreed upon. Nerves must be setting in with the wedding only twenty-four hours away.

After she was back at the castle, Madeleine kept thinking about the not-quite-a-kiss that left her…unsatisfied. She'd wanted more.

Why?

A knock interrupted her thoughts.

She opened the door to see Enrique standing there.

Her heart bumped.

He was so handsome in his charcoal gray suit, white shirt, and yellow tie. "Ready for dinner?"

Madeleine would have rather eaten alone with Enrique, but the dinner was in their honor, so they had to show up or her mother would throw a fit worse than little Penelope had in the vestibule. "I am."

"My father arrived. Alejandro and Jules are here, and her brother, Brandt, too. King Alaric and his wife made other plans for dinner, but everyone has settled into their guest suites on the other side of the castle."

Madeleine wasn't surprised the king and queen of Aliestle skipped dinner. This was their first visit to Gaullia in decades. "What about Prince Niko and Princess Izzy?"

"They are downstairs," Enrique said. "King

Dmitar and Queen Beatrice send their regrets. They are at the hotel with their three grandchildren."

Madeleine laughed. "Smart choice."

"They'll have more fun than us."

"Until you head out with your brother and three crown princes for your last hurrah as a single man," she teased.

Enrique's jaw jutted forward. "I don't have to go out."

"Yes, you do." She touched his arm. "I was joking. It's a tradition."

"It doesn't have to be mine."

"I want you to go."

"You'll be here alone."

"I don't mind."

His gaze darkened. "What if I do?"

"Karl planned this for you." He'd never had the chance to do it for Louie. "If I had a problem with it, I'd let you know. Please, go."

A beat passed. And another. "You can text. Or call me tonight."

He was trying to be so serious, but he was too cute, trying not to upset her. "Thanks, but I plan to go to bed early so I look beautiful tomorrow."

"You are always beautiful." His cheeks turned pink.

"Thank you," she said before he fumbled with what to say next. He didn't do well when he backtracked.

He swallowed. "You're welcome."

Her gaze locked on his. He opened his mouth, but no words came out.

Everything stopped. Her feet. Time. Even her heart seemed to have stilled.

He raised his arm, brought his hand to her face, and ran the edge of his finger along her cheek. His light touch sparked something deep inside her. His lips were mere inches away. She wanted a real kiss to make up for the one in the cathedral.

All she had to do was…

Madeleine lifted her chin. She rose on her tiptoes, bringing her mouth to his.

The initial touch brought a shock. An explosion of tingles followed. Warmth came next.

Only a second must have passed, but his kiss heated her blood, taking it from simmering to sizzling. Her toes curled. She arched against him, needing more. Oh, so much more.

Of his taste, of his scent, of his warmth.

With her lips against his, nothing else mattered. The empty places inside her filled. The missing pieces found.

Someone coughed.

She jumped away from Enrique. Her rapid breathing matched her heart rate.

"You're late for dinner." Karl appeared to be trying not to laugh. "Mother sent me to find you."

Oh, no. What have I done?

Kissing Enrique like that made no sense. Yet she'd been compelled to do it. Had that been a mistake?

Madeleine glanced his way.

Confusion clouded his gaze, but his mouth curved upward.

Did that mean he wasn't upset? Or had he enjoyed the kiss, too?

Thinking about how she'd taken the initiative caused her cheeks to burn.

"Mads?" Karl asked.

That jolted her out of her thoughts. "We're on our way."

Enrique straightened his tie. "Yes. We were—"

"Don't make an excuse or give a reason," Karl counseled. "My mother will see right through that."

"It's true," Madeleine agreed. "But we couldn't help that we were delayed."

A lopsided grin formed on her brother's face. "Is delayed a synonym for a hot kiss?"

The kiss had been hot. She swallowed. Better than the first one at the cathedral. She tried to put that one behind her. That was why she'd wanted another kiss today. Why she'd been driven toward Enrique.

A new kiss to replace the first one.

Enrique laughed. "If it is, I won't mind being delayed longer."

More heat flooded her face because she wouldn't mind that herself.

Should she want more?

Self-preservation shouted *no*, except her lips screamed yes. Her stomach sank. A proper princess knew the correct answer. But what if it didn't match what she wanted?

Chapter Sixteen

After the delicious dinner ended, Enrique wanted to ask Madeleine about the unexpected kiss in the hallway, but Alejandro, Karl, Niko, and Brandt had whisked Enrique out of the castle. The princes piled into a limousine. Captain Mendoza sat in the passenger seat. An SUV containing the other bodyguards and security team followed them.

"Where are we going?" Enrique asked to be polite. He was resigned that tonight was happening.

Alejandro, seated next to him, shrugged. "Karl made the plans."

"And they are top secret," Gaullia's crown prince teased. "Only the driver and our security teams know the destination."

Brandt removed a bottle of top-shelf whiskey from the limo's bar. "Anyone up for pre-gaming?"

Everyone, except Enrique, was. Brandt passed out the glasses.

Karl raised his. "To Enrique. May the future king of La Isla de la Aurora be blessed with a happy marriage and more hot kisses from my sister."

"I'll drink to that." Niko downed his shot.

The others did the same. Brandt refilled glasses.

Alejandro eyed Enrique curiously. "Hot kisses, huh?"

Enrique's face heated. He was thankful for the dim lights in the limousine. No one would notice.

Karl snickered. "Why do you think they were late to dinner?"

Being the only sober one would make for a longer night. "Give me a drink."

"The groom's going wild, gentlemen." Brandt filled another glass and handed it over. The crown prince of Aliestle had a frat-boy vibe about him. He was the opposite of his tyrannical father. Brandt raised his glass. "To hot kisses from hot princesses."

Madeleine was hot. She was also intelligent, well-spoken, kind, and gorgeous. Enrique downed his whiskey. The liquid burned going down, but he couldn't deny the quality.

Brandt poured more whiskey into the glasses.

"My turn." Niko lifted his whiskey. "May hot kisses lead to little princes and princesses."

As the others drank, Enrique imagined a pregnant Madeleine. That wouldn't be happening right away, but he couldn't wait to start a family with her. He gulped his shot.

"One more." Brandt filled each glass again. "Then we'll be warmed up."

Alejandro stared at Enrique over the lip of his glass. "May the hot kisses multiply each year of your marriage and your reign."

From your lips to God's ear.

Enrique drank. The whiskey warmed and loosened him.

"Hear, hear." Karl tossed back his drink before glancing out the side window. "Perfect timing. We've arrived."

It was a small bar located in the bottom of an old windmill. Artwork hung on stone walls. Leather chairs were tucked around dark wood tables.

"Where is everyone?" Brandt asked.

"I reserved the place," Karl admitted. "This way wannabe princesses won't disturb us."

"Speak for yourself." Brandt took a swig from the now empty whiskey bottle. "I enjoy what a wannabe princess will do for a shot at wearing a crown jewel on her ring finger."

"My brother-in-law aside…" Alejandro slapped

Karl on the back. "Good idea."

"Thank you, Karl." Enrique assumed Madeleine had told her brother a private outing would be better. She truly was perfect for him. And if more kisses like tonight's followed…

As a wide smile spread across his face, he sat.

Alejandro nudged him. "Thinking about your bride?"

Enrique nodded.

The other men sat, except for Brandt who remained standing.

"Who wants to check out their liquor offerings?" Jules's brother asked.

Alejandro rolled his eyes. "You want to check out the redheaded bartender."

"I do." He appeared proud not sorry. "I'm betrothed to a girl who prefers éclairs over me, but until I'm wearing a ring, I'll do as I please."

"Madeleine enjoys éclairs," Enrique said.

Niko laughed. "The groom has it bad."

"My sister loves éclairs, but you're correct." Karl shook his head. "Enrique does have it bad."

A server placed five pints of ale on the table.

Enrique took a sip. The beer tasted a touch bitter and full of hops.

"Your arranged marriage is turning into a love match." Alejandro sounded pleased. "This is what you wanted."

"Yes," Enrique admitted. "But she's not there."

Niko set his beer down. "I was the slacker with me and Izzy, but it didn't take too long for me to realize I'd fallen in love with my wife."

Enrique sighed. Madeleine loving him would be a dream come true. "I'm hopeful she'll come around."

"They have darts," Niko said.

Alejandro stood. "I'm game."

The two men walked to the dartboard, leaving Enrique with Karl.

Enrique took another sip of his beer. "Is something wrong?"

"You're in love with Madeleine."

Was he? Enrique stared into his glass. "I've never been in love, but I've never felt like this about any woman except your sister. She told me about Louie and how she doesn't want a love match, but that doesn't matter. It won't stop me from spending every day of our life together, showing her how much I care about her. I hope someday she'll feel the same way about me."

Karl took a long, slow sip from his glass. "Louie was my closest friend. He wasn't perfect."

"No one is."

Karl drank again—this time a gulp. "He did things my sister doesn't know about. I never had a reason to tell her until now, but if she knew the truth—"

"No." The word shot out of Enrique's mouth with a ferocity that startled him.

"She'll be able to move on. Fall in love—"

"No," he repeated. "I understand what you're doing, Karl. I appreciate it. But please don't tarnish Louie's memory or Madeleine's love for him. She'll either love me or not, but that needs to happen naturally. Love can't be forced nor do I want her hurting, thinking she's wasted the past five years."

"You love her." Karl gave a light-hearted laugh. "What you said proves it. She'll come around."

"There's no rush. I promised to give her time, and I will. I just pray she gets there, eventually."

"She will. You're a good guy. I didn't like you at first," Karl admitted. "But you've proven yourself worthy of her."

Pride swelled. Contentment, too. The kiss tonight had been the start. Her brother's words told Enrique he was ready for the next step. "Thank you."

"Want to play darts?" Karl asked.

Enrique rose. "Lead the way."

Madeleine stared at her bed. Going to sleep made the most sense with the wedding tomorrow, but she wasn't tired. She couldn't stop wondering what Enrique was doing with Alejandro, Karl, Niko, and Brandt.

A stag—or bachelor, as Izzy said Americans called it—party?

Madeleine's stomach churned. She didn't blame

Enrique for a final night of fun. She just missed him.

She needed to occupy herself. Not television. Nor an embroidery project. Her books had been packed for her move to La Isla de la Aurora, but she could read a novel on her cell phone. Only that didn't appeal to her, either.

She sighed. "What am I supposed to do the night before my wedding?"

Madeleine hadn't gotten this far with her first engagement.

Widowed before she was a bride.

Not the most pleasant thought, but that reminded her.

"Wait. I'm not alone tonight." She headed to the nightstand where she removed Louie's photograph and placed the frame on her dresser in the same place it had sat until her father arranged her match. "Forgive me, my love."

Not for getting married. That was one of her duties.

But for laughing and having fun with Enrique. For being in his arms and kissing him back. For realizing marriage to him wouldn't be the second worst thing that could happen to her.

"I've been so torn. Between my life with you and my life without you." She traced Louie's smile. "I miss you so much, but until I met Enrique, I hadn't realized how lonely I've been. He makes me happy. Hopeful for the future once more. I never believed I would feel this way again. But no matter what happens, my love for you will remain. I love you. I always will."

Out the window in the distance, spotlights shined on the fountain. So much would change tomorrow.

"Enrique offered to have your fountain repaired. I told him to go ahead. The fountain is too beautiful to sit unused. But I won't be here to see it working again, not until I visit. Which I will. As soon as I can. It depends on what my duties will be."

Madeleine was still debating whether she could bring Louie's photo with her to the island. She should discuss it with Enrique, but she would wait until after the wedding.

There was, however, one thing she wouldn't—couldn't—leave behind. She pulled the necklace from beneath her blouse, took off her engagement ring, removed Louie's ring from the chain, and slid it on her finger.

"Even if I no longer wear your ring every day, it will never be far from me." She kissed the engraved signet. "I promise."

Her breath hitched.

When they were teenagers, they'd promised to love each other forever. She'd been trying to do that. Duty, however, was getting in the way. At least she could keep this new promise.

She squeezed the ring tightly. "Promise."

Madeleine had built her life around Louie. He became her everything, her world. The older she got, the more time she spent with him. Friends became secondary until they no longer contacted her.

After he'd died, she hadn't reconnected with what friends remained. Truth was, they'd been Louie's friends first and being around them was too painful. She had her family. That was all she'd needed at the time, especially Karl. Except the weeks had turned into months. Those became years. Even at graduate school, she'd kept to herself. And now…

She'd spent five years missing Louie. Mourning him.

That explained why she was alone in her bedroom the night before her wedding. And why a bridal tea hadn't been thrown. Oh, her mother had offered, but Madeleine said no because she didn't want acquaintances—okay, strangers—attending out of obligation. The engagement party had been difficult enough.

She touched the glass covering the photograph. "I suppose now that I'm getting married, it's time to make friends of my own."

A knock sounded. "I'm coming."

As she padded across the room, her bare feet sank into the ornate rug. She opened the door.

Jules held a bottle of wine and three glasses. Izzy carried a plate covered with a silver lid. Both women dressed casually in leggings and T-shirts, opposite from their lovely gowns at the formal dinner earlier.

"Surprise!" the two shouted in unison.

"Um, hi." Uncertain, Madeleine tightened her grip on the doorknob.

Jules flashed an encouraging smile. "There wasn't a bachelorette party or a bridal luncheon on the daily schedule so Enrique suggested we have a wedding eve girls' night."

Madeleine startled. "Enrique?"

Jules nodded, her gaze softening. "He didn't want you to miss out on any wedding traditions."

Madeleine's heart bumped. Enrique was always thinking of her.

"And we didn't want you to be alone," Izzy added, her accent one hundred percent American, which made sense because she'd been raised in North Carolina. "Unless you have other plans…"

"I don't." The words flew out. Madeleine was grateful for the company. She opened the door wider. "Please, come in."

Jules entered first, heading to the overstuffed loveseat and chair near the fireplace. She set the glasses on the small coffee table, pulled out the cork, and poured the white wine. "I had the bottle opened by one of the kitchen staff."

Madeleine sat in the chair, leaving the loveseat for the two women, whom she knew were close friends. "Smart thinking because I don't have a wine opener in my room."

Laughing, Jules handed out the glasses. "I didn't think you would, because Enrique says you're a proper princess."

Madeleine raised her wine. "Is there any other kind?"

"I doubt being called a perfect princess is any better." Jules took a sip.

"Better than a reluctant one," Izzy joked. "That's what Niko called me. I had no idea I was royalty until he showed up at the garage where I worked."

"You're so lucky to have experienced a normal childhood." Madeleine stiffened. "I—"

"We understand," Izzy interrupted, compassion filling her eyes. "Jules more than me, but being a princess isn't for the faint of heart."

Jules nodded. "Especially when a handsome prince is involved."

Izzy shook her head. "Says the princess who was engaged to my husband and Madeleine's groom."

"Not by choice," Jules countered. "Besides, my engagement to Niko was never formalized with a contract. And Enrique and I have never been more than friends. We never did more than hold hands. He may have kissed my cheek…"

"It's okay." Madeleine stared at the beautiful woman. "You don't owe me any explanation."

"I want you to understand there was nothing between us." Lines creased Jules's forehead. "Just as Niko and I were never more than friends."

"My husband wanted her dowry and the connections aligning with Aliestle would bring," Izzy said in a matter-of-fact tone.

"So did Enrique." As Madeleine took a drink of her wine, both princesses stared at her with wide eyes. "What?"

"You've talked about this?" Jules sounded surprised.

"Yes, he's been open about his past. As I have with mine."

"Good." Izzy swirled the wine in her glass. "Communication is key."

Jules nodded. "It's necessary for a successful marriage."

"So are heirs," Madeleine mumbled. She didn't know why she said that because she hadn't drunk enough wine to be tipsy. "I mean…"

She didn't know what to say next.

"It's okay to be nervous about your wedding night," Izzy said. "I was. Have you and Enrique discussed sex and children?"

Jules shot her friend a warning. "Izzy…"

Izzy shook her head. "I became pregnant with twins on our honeymoon. It happens so it should be discussed before the kissing begins and the clothes come off."

Madeleine's cheeks heated. Maybe once she was married, talking so openly would be easy, but sex wasn't something she'd discussed—beyond the bare essentials her mother explained—with anyone.

"You're embarrassing our beautiful bride." Jules

stared over the lip of her wineglass. "Don't worry about Enrique. He's been called everything from selfish to pompous but never a player or womanizer. All he wants to do is please those he cares about, especially his father. That's made him appear standoffish and self-centered, but he's not. Enrique will never force you into anything you're not ready for or don't want."

"Though you may be surprised how…eager you find yourself," Izzy added.

Madeleine managed not to spew a mouthful of chardonnay over herself and the chair. "Ours is an arranged match. He'll do what's required. As I will. Out of duty."

Except her words weren't one hundred percent true. She didn't feel that way any longer.

"Arranged marriages aren't the worst thing in the world." Izzy sat cross-legged. "Jules once told me just because you don't love someone at the beginning doesn't mean feelings won't develop. Love can grow. It did for me and Niko. I can't imagine life without him."

Madeleine's gaze traveled to Louie's photograph. "Falling in love again scares me."

"Do you think you'll ever love someone like you did Louie?" Jules asked, no judgment in her voice.

Once upon a time, Madeleine's answer would have been a firm *no*. Now…

"I don't know," she admitted. "I respect Enrique's

sense of duty to his family and country. He's so kind, always putting me first. But losing Louie…"

"It changed you," Izzy finished for her.

Madeleine nodded. "We had our future planned. Now he's gone, and I'm here to go on without him. Being a wife and mother will give me a purpose that has been missing. I care about Enrique."

Jules grinned. "Wonderful, because he's falling in love with you."

Madeleine's heart soared. A part of her wanted to fall in love, too. And then, she remembered…Louie. A battle between the past and the present—of what she'd had and what she wanted—raged inside her.

"Enrique can't be falling in love." She fought a rising panic. "We barely know each other."

He also knows I'm still in love with Louie.

"Love doesn't follow a timeframe. It doesn't occur at the same time with a couple, either. I fell for Niko first," Izzy admitted.

No. This wasn't possible. Enrique had told her he understood, but if it were true…

Madeleine's hands shook. She set her glass on the table. "What if I never fall in love with him?"

"Love takes many forms," Jules said evenly. "There's the love between husband and wife. The love of a parent for a child. The love between friends. And the love of two people determined to do what's best for their country and its future."

Times spent with Enrique flashed in Madeleine's

mind. He'd stopped talking about his heart being broken and unable to love. He'd been so focused on her, but she thought that was because he wanted her to marry him. "What if I can't love him how he wants?"

"You said you were honest with him." Jules refilled her wineglass. "Enrique is a smart man. He understands."

He'd told Madeleine he did, but…

His sweet kisses. The way his gaze softened. The tender stroke of his fingertips.

Did he understand? Or was she leading him on? Responding not as a woman missing her dead love but as a woman, yearning for the touch of the man she would marry?

She swallowed. "We discussed our situation and Louie, but then some things happened."

Izzy blew out a breath. "We may need more wine."

As Jules arched an eyebrow, her expression tightened. "What things?"

Madeleine's cheeks burned. "Kisses."

"Enrique won't mistake kisses for anything more," Jules said, sounding relieved.

"I'm sorry. I'm confused about my own feelings." Madeleine slumped in the chair. "I fear I'm overthinking everything."

Izzy nodded. "That happens, especially on the night before a wedding."

"To a man you hadn't met until a month ago," Jules added.

"Try two weeks." Madeleine rubbed the back of her neck to ease the knots forming. That was too soon to fall in love, wasn't it?

"You know what we forgot?" Jules lifted the silver lid covering the plate. "Dessert."

Izzy leaned forward. "Oh, I love éclairs."

Warmth flowed through Madeleine. Someone, most likely Enrique, must have mentioned her favorite dessert. "They are the best."

"Before we put our calories on, I want to make a toast." Izzy raised her wineglass. "To charming princes, dreamy castles, and happily ever afters."

The first two were givens. Madeleine had stopped believing in the third, but could it be possible?

She tapped her glass against the other two. A chime hung in the air. "I'll drink to that."

Happy ending or not, having Enrique by her side would be better than the way she'd been living these past five years.

Chapter Seventeen

When Enrique arrived back at the castle, he headed to his room, slightly buzzed but happier than ever. He was glad he'd gone out tonight. The men thought Enrique and Madeleine made a good match. That she wasn't indifferent to him. That love was possible.

Remembering her kiss, he touched his mouth.

Karl was correct.

Enrique had fallen in love with his princess bride. He loved Madeleine. Loved her mind, body, and soul. She wasn't ready to love him, but his love for her was strong enough to get them through until she caught up.

With Madeleine at his side, all his dreams would come true.

She was what he'd wished to find.

He hurried to her bedroom.

It hurt not being able to tell her how he felt, but he could ask for a kiss. That wouldn't be too much, especially if seeing her before he went to bed would help him sleep better. He glanced at the time.

It wasn't that late.

His heart pounding in his chest, he knocked on her door.

He hadn't understood the depths of his feelings for her before, but now he did. Giddiness welled inside him.

This is what being in love feels like.

Her door opened. A sole lamp illuminated the room, but the light from the hallway allowed him to see her.

Her unglossed lips parted but no sound came out. Her hair—tangled from sleep—fell past her shoulders. She wore no makeup. But she'd never been more beautiful.

Her robe's belt was tied around her waist. Ever the proper princess—even in the middle of the night.

"It's late." His voice sounded deeper, unrecognizable. He cleared his throat. "But I had to see you."

She motioned for him to come in but didn't close

the door behind him.

"Are you okay?" she asked.

"Yes. I've never been better." He tried to keep from fidgeting from excitement because he couldn't let on how he felt. Asking for a kiss would be enough. "I wanted…"

The lamp on her nightstand caught his attention. He noticed a framed photograph next to it.

Louie.

Enrique's chest tightened. Air rushed from his lungs.

Madeleine had been honest about her love for Louie. One picture wasn't a big deal. Her past didn't matter.

No sense acting silly or juvenile out of jealousy. Yet misgivings formed, quadrupling by the second.

Madeleine touched his arm. "What is it?"

His gaze traveled to her left hand, to the gold ring she wore. Not the one he'd given her, and that she'd worn during dinner.

This was the same ring she wore around her neck.

Close to her heart.

Louie's ring.

She was wearing it the night before her wedding.

Enrique's heart cracked. The feeling was so physical he was surprised she hadn't heard the organ splitting in two.

He stepped back.

Madeleine's brows drew together. "What did you

want to say?"

Emotion clogged his throat. He'd come to ask for a kiss. A good thing he hadn't admitted his love with a foolish declaration.

Stupid. Idiotic.

She'd told him about Louie.

Can you accept that my heart belongs to another and always will?

Yes, because I never expected to marry for love.

Enrique had accepted that she still grieved and needed time. He'd been fine doing that, but his heart hadn't given up on finding love.

With her.

In the future.

Only Madeleine hadn't meant she would move on at some point. She meant she would love Louie and no one else.

Enrique wasn't fine with that.

He couldn't be.

Not when he remembered his parents before their divorce. Marriage was difficult enough with two people. Add in a third…

Forget it.

Competing with a ghost for Madeleine's affection—a perfect ghost in her heart and mind— would never work.

Enrique couldn't win. He didn't even want to try.

And he knew what he had to do.

They may have agreed to marry, but she was being

forced into this royal union. The same as him.

The only difference was he now wanted to marry her. Not to save his chance at being king, but because he loved her. Whereas she…

She didn't want the marriage.

Or him.

She was everything he wanted, everything he hadn't known he needed, but that wasn't enough. He would never be enough for her to love because her heart wanted Louie.

Pressure built inside him, ready to erupt like a fiery volcano. But he wouldn't give in. He couldn't lose control.

Enrique wanted Madeleine to be happy. More than he wanted anything else. Even if her happiness meant he lost everything, he had to give her an out.

"Please tell me what's going on," she urged, her voice tense.

He tried to organize his jumbled thoughts. One breath followed another. "I can't force you to marry me."

There. He'd said it. And the sentence had made sense.

Her hand dropped from his arm. "I don't understand. We signed the marriage contract. The wedding is tomorrow."

"That's why I'm giving you the chance to back out before it's too late."

"Did you change your mind? Did I do something?"

The words tumbled out of her mouth.

"No, you've been wonderful. But your father arranged this match. You deserve better. Time so you can continue to heal." Enrique kept talking before he lost his nerve. "I'll take the blame, cancel everything, shoulder any responsibility, and pay whatever costs."

"Oh, Enrique." She took his hands in hers.

He steeled himself for her to say she agreed with his plan.

She squeezed his arm. "I don't want an out."

The tension, however, didn't leave his body. "Marrying me isn't what you want."

"I never said that."

Not in so many words, but the signs were on her nightstand and on her finger. "You are doing your duty."

Nothing more.

"This never was meant to be what I want or what you want." Her tone was steady and calm. "Our marriage is for our families, our people, and our countries."

He understood their families wanted this for their own reasons, but… "What do your country and people have to do with this?"

She released his hands, her arms falling to her sides, and stared at the carpet.

He raised her chin with his fingertip. "Please tell me."

"They…we…need protection from Aliestle."

His father had handled the marriage contract negotiations. Enrique assumed the benefits for Gaullia were financial, but this made no sense. "What kind of protection?"

"Our treasury borrowed money from Aliestle, never expecting King Alaric would call for full repayment of the loan. He's threatening to take our land if we don't pay. Marrying you…"

"Provides an alliance with Aliestle."

"A tentative one, but that's more than we have now."

"I didn't know." That explained why King Leon had approached his father. It was a reason for many arrangements over the centuries.

"Do you hate me for using our marriage in this way?" she asked, her voice full of regret.

"I could never hate you. I want to make you happy."

"Then marry me as we'd planned. Helping Gaullia remain intact means everything to me." The determined set of her jaw told him that was true.

Enrique's hopes shattered. His dream for the marriage he'd wanted with her was over before it began, but he wouldn't abandon Madeleine or her country. "I will marry you per the contract."

She exhaled as if she'd been holding her breath. "Thank you."

"Under the circumstances, our union should be in name only. That will give Gaullia the protection you seek."

And keep my heart from being hurt more.

Her face scrunched. "But heirs—"

"Alejandro and Jules will provide those," Enrique interrupted. He was barely holding himself together. "The marriage contract stipulates if no heirs are born within five years, we are free to divorce. That gives us time to figure out a way for Gaullia to repay Aliestle so your country is safe."

Madeleine's lower lip quivered. "I thought you wanted a wife."

The urge to comfort her was strong. Enrique needed to be stronger, but he would allow himself one last touch while they were alone. He cupped the side of her face. "I want what is best for you. I want you to be happy."

Her eyes gleamed. "You've made me happy."

Then he'd done the right thing. Even if he…hurt.

As he lowered his hand, she leaned forward.

Enrique pressed his arms against his sides. One touch was enough. He didn't dare allow himself more, especially a hug.

"Tomorrow is a big day." He wanted to hold her, but he stepped away. "Sleep, my princess."

"You, too." Her voice was whisper-soft.

Not trusting his voice, he nodded.

After he left her room, he closed the door behind him. The click of the latch sealed his fate—being married to the woman he loved but never being with her in the way he wanted.

Staring at the closed door, he imagined her crawling into bed with a smile on her face.

Sleep wouldn't come easy for him, if at all.

He'd wanted to prove his mother wrong, and he had. He had fallen in love. His heart worked fine. Only now it had splintered into a million different pieces, each jagged and raw and slicing him to bits.

Yes, he'd gotten his wish, but he should have wished for one thing more—for someone to love him in return.

Because now he was worse off than before.

Enrique trudged to his room.

How was he going to survive being so close to her when he loved her so much?

She would never be his.

Or he hers.

Enrique stopped.

He couldn't do it.

Couldn't live with Madeleine, be married to her, and only be friends.

Which meant he needed a new plan.

Think, think, think.

An idea formed and then crystalized in his mind.

It wasn't what he'd wanted, but he had no choice.

He bypassed his bedroom door, headed to another, and knocked.

"Who is it?" his father called out.

"It's Enrique." He squared his shoulders, knowing

A middle-of-the-night meeting with three kings, three crown princes, one royal aide who was also an attorney, his brother, and his sister-in-law wasn't where Enrique expected to be, but he would do anything to help Madeleine.

Initially, heated words filled the room. But after everyone had spoken—well, yelled—honest negotiations began. The civility didn't ease his aching heart, but it helped.

Jovan, who was Prince Niko's aide, glanced up from his laptop. "The agreement is printing."

"Thank you for your help," Enrique said to the man, whom he hadn't met until tonight.

The two from Vernonia weren't involved, but their presence had been vital to the success of the meeting and more than once, Niko had been a calming source.

His father touched Enrique's shoulder. "Are you certain this is what you want, my son?"

No. But what Enrique wanted wasn't possible.

"Yes, sir." The ache in his chest intensified, but he pushed past it. He would have to get used to the pain and emptiness threatening to swamp him. "I am content knowing Gaullia's financial issues are under control and the island is in safe hands."

He didn't mention the real reason behind this agreement—Madeleine. As long as her country was safe from Aliestle, he would be—not happy—satisfied, knowing she no longer had to worry or be forced into a marriage she didn't want.

Alejandro scowled at him, but respect and affection gleamed in his eyes. "You've shown yourself to be a king tonight. More so than any of us in the room. I am proud to call you brother."

Brandt nodded. "I second that, my friend."

"Third," Karl added. "It isn't every day a crown prince willingly gives up the throne to save another country on the brink of financial ruin and ensure the monarchy continues in his own."

The three actual kings remained silent, but none appeared to disagree with Karl's words.

"I agree." Niko focused on Enrique. "You are welcome in Vernonia if you need a place to…regroup."

"Thank you." Enrique had been driven by a purpose he didn't understand. He'd like to say he was being selfless, but this agreement negotiated among the three countries was as much for him as it was for Madeleine.

Now that a marriage contract no longer tied them together, he could put needed distance between them. "But no praise is required. I am only doing what is necessary."

"Exactly." Alejandro sounded exasperated. "Which is why the throne should be yours. If you marry before Father retires—"

"No, bro." Enrique used the word his brother had goaded him with for years. Only he spoke with affection and gratitude. Perhaps someday he would fall in love again. But that wouldn't be anytime soon, which meant Alejandro would be king. The hollowness in Enrique's chest, however, had more to do with Madeleine than relinquishing his title. "That will not happen. This isn't the life you planned…"

Jules held onto Alejandro's hand. "We will be fine. You're the one making the sacrifice."

Enrique shot a glance toward King Alaric. "Your father might disagree."

The larger-than-life man laughed. "I still get my money albeit later than I'd like, and my daughter is to be queen. No complaints from where I'm sitting, but you have surprised me, Enrique. In a good way."

"I feel the same." King Leon sat behind his desk. "You are Gaullia's hero."

Enrique didn't want to be a hero. He wanted to be Madeleine's husband. "Thank you, sir."

"You've helped our financial situation when I thought we'd exhausted our options," King Leon added. "And you've freed my daughter from a marriage she didn't want."

The last words sliced into Enrique's heart. He forced himself not to react when he could have easily doubled over in pain if he allowed himself the luxury.

But her father was correct.

She didn't want Enrique.

She didn't love him.

They were better off apart so she could finish grieving. Eventually, she would find someone to love who would allow her to move on with her life. She deserved more than being stuck in the past, focused on her first and only love.

"Then we are all in agreement," his father stated with a hint of sadness in his voice. "Aliestle will lower payments and extend the loan due date by ten years. La Isla de la Aurora will provide collateral in case Gaullia falters with future payments. When Alejandro is coronated—"

"*If*, not when, sir," Alejandro corrected.

"Pardon me," their father said. "If Alejandro is coronated, one hundred million of Gaullia's debt to Aliestle will be forgiven, and twenty-five million donated to our island's educational initiative."

The first amount had been the dowry offered by King Alaric to make his daughter queen of La Isla de la Aurora. Enrique had dreamed of how the money could improve the island, but now the payment would help the woman he loved. The second amount would be a legacy to his beloved country, one he would entrust to his family, one he would miss with his entire being.

"Then it's settled." King Alaric's deep voice echoed through the office.

The kings shook hands, a gentlemen's agreement to seal their legal one.

"What will you do now?" Karl asked.

Drink? No, Enrique had learned his lesson. And crying never helped. He'd tried that before, too.

"I'm not sure. The island doesn't need a former prince hanging around as it transitions to a new ruler." He was a man without a country, a home, or a job. "My work experience isn't typical, but I have an MBA. Putting distance between myself and this continent makes the most sense. Perhaps see what America or Canada offers."

Both his father's and brother's faces fell. Their eyes gleamed with unshed tears.

Their reaction surprised Enrique. But then again, he'd caught them off guard. They hadn't known of his plan not to return to the island. But they would see his leaving was for the best.

His father parted his lips, but Enrique couldn't handle anything else. Not tonight.

Even though he wanted to collapse, he kept his head high. "Wherever I go, whatever I do, I will be fine."

Not at first. Most likely not for a while. But eventually he would be okay because he had no other choice.

Chapter Eighteen

Sunlight streamed into Madeleine's room, but she was already awake. She'd slept fitfully, tossing and turning, mulling over what Enrique had said about the marriage he now wanted with her.

She wouldn't be his wife. Not in the way most defined marriage.

Her forehead throbbed.

Why did he want that?

For days—weeks before they'd met if she were being honest—an in-name-only marriage was what she'd wanted. A state marriage, a business arrangement, nothing more. But now…

Something ate at her. Had led to a restless night. Knotted her stomach.

She stared at Louie's photograph. "This is what I wanted originally. Why aren't I happier?"

Her question remained unanswered. Like all the ones she'd asked the photograph for the past five years.

Five years.

One. Two. Three. Four. Five.

That was how long Louie had been gone. How long a part of her heart had been missing. How long her and Enrique's "marriage in name only" would last.

She would be thirty-two. Not old. But then what?

She'd stopped thinking about the future when Louie died, but this week she'd started again. Imagining a life with Enrique. Dreaming of their children.

Now none of that would happen.

When their marriage ended, what would she do?

Return to this room at the castle? Spend the rest of her life talking to a photograph? Keep wishing for that elusive happy ending?

Because her future had been headed in that direction before Enrique arrived in Gaullia. But she no longer wanted that. She wanted…

Him.

Once they were husband and wife, she would convince him to return to their original agreement. Until then, all she could do was get ready for the wedding.

Madeleine showered and then put on her robe. Preparations should start soon. She walked into her bedroom.

Empty.

Where was everyone?

Lilia hadn't brought her breakfast.

None of the hair and makeup artists had arrived.

A knock sounded.

Finally.

Madeleine straightened her robe. "Come in."

Her parents entered. Karl followed. All three had wide smiles. Of course, they did. After today, Gaullia would be safe.

"Good morning." She peered around her brother to see who else was behind them. No one was there. "Where is the team who is supposed to be turning me into a beautiful bride?"

Her mother laughed. "You're beautiful as you are, dear."

Nodding, her father stared at Madeleine. "The team isn't coming because I called off the wedding."

Madeleine gasped. Her hand flew to her chest. Tears streamed from her eyes. "Enrique knows what's at stake. He said he would marry me. Why would he—"

"Enrique saved us," Karl interrupted, sounding happy. "And you."

Madeleine searched the faces of her parents and brother. She saw no worry or stress. Their smiles hadn't wavered. "I don't understand."

"Enrique didn't want to force you into an arranged marriage," her father explained. "He said you needed more time to grieve Louie."

That didn't clear up her confusion. Enrique knew how she felt about Louie. They'd discussed that the day they'd met. "This still makes no sense."

"Enrique wants you to be happy," Karl explained. "That's why he gathered everyone together last night. He negotiated an agreement to pay off our debt to Aliestle so you wouldn't have to get married."

Her mouth fell open. "King Alaric agreed?"

"He did," her father said. "The renegotiated loan has more favorable terms."

Beaming, Karl nodded. "To top it off, when Julianna becomes queen, one hundred million of what we owe will be wiped out."

Wait. That, too, made no sense. "How will Jules be queen? Alejandro isn't the crown prince."

Her father's gaze darkened. "Their country's Parliament changed the rules of succession. A crown prince must be married to become king."

The air rushed from her lungs. A weight pressed against her chest. "Enrique never told me."

"Few knew. That was the reason for the rush to get married." Karl shook his head. "I misjudged the guy. Enrique might not be a smooth conversationalist in social situations, but he's the definition of selfless. He helped us, but in doing so, he must relinquish his title."

She'd seen that selfless side of Enrique. Still…

"Why?" Her voice was whisper-soft. "I don't understand why he did this."

"Your brother told you why," her mother said. "Enrique cares about you. He wants you to be happy."

I want what is best for you. I want you to be happy.

He'd said that to her last night, but the visit had been odd. He'd entered her room bouncing with excitement. Then, something had changed. His expression. His entire demeanor.

But what? Had he seen something?

Her gaze landed on the photograph of Louie.

His photo still sat next to her bed from the night before.

She wore Louie's ring on her left hand.

Not Enrique's.

Her stomach hardened. "Oh, no."

This was her fault. He must have seen them. Add in what she'd said to him, and he'd taken the steps he thought she wanted.

Warmth tingled in her arms and legs before spreading and settling around her heart. No one had sacrificed so much for her.

Not her parents. Not her brother. Not Louie.

Those people had known her for years, but Enrique hadn't needed years to know what she wanted—needed. He'd just known. And made it happen. Even if doing so meant giving up everything he wanted and loved.

Love.

Madeleine crossed her arms in front of herself.

She loved him.

Somehow he'd found his way into her heart. Not in the same first blush of love as Louie had. No, her love for Enrique was built on a foundation of friendship and respect and…attraction. That was why she'd been upset last night. She wanted a real marriage with him.

She wanted everything with him.

How could she have been so blind to her heart?

But she knew the reason—fear.

Louie wasn't getting in the way. She was.

She'd been afraid to love. Afraid to be the one left behind again. Only that was happening anyway.

Because she'd been too scared to admit her feelings to herself, let alone Enrique.

Madeleine didn't know whether to laugh or cry, but the hole in her heart grew bigger. "What will Enrique do now?"

"Don't worry," her mother said. "He's a grown man. He'll know what to do."

Karl nodded. "Enrique said he would be fine."

"He mentioned heading to America or Canada," her father added.

Of course Enrique would say those things. Because he was putting everyone else first, but she knew better.

Knew *him* better.

Madeleine pushed back her shoulders. "I need to

see him."

"I'm sorry, dear." Her mother touched Madeleine's arm. "He was leaving for the airport this morning."

No! Heart pounding, Madeleine ran to his room. The door was open, and maids were cleaning it. "Where is Prince Enrique?"

"He left, ma'am," one said.

No. No. No.

Madeleine hadn't been able to do anything to keep from losing Louie, but she wasn't about to lose Enrique. She sprinted to the staircase, not caring her hair was damp, her feet were bare, and she wore only a robe. She hadn't run since boarding school when she'd been on the track team, but she poured every ounce of strength into her legs.

Please don't let me be too late.

A uniformed guard opened one of the front doors.

She dashed outside where Enrique was getting into a limousine. "Stop."

He straightened and then turned. A confused expression crossed his face, but then he pressed his lips together, staring at her as if she were a unicorn.

She met his gaze full-on. "You called off our wedding."

He said nothing, but a vein at his jaw pulsed. His hands balled into fists and then he flexed his fingers.

Madeleine's parents had raised her to be proper. Her family's definition meant being reserved and polite. But she couldn't be those things now.

She took a step toward Enrique. The cobblestone beneath her feet was rough, but she didn't care.

"You're leaving without saying goodbye." Her voice didn't hold the power she hoped, but she was struggling to breathe.

Enrique raised his chin slightly. "Your father told me he would explain the situation."

Even though she wanted to run to him and beg him to stay or take her with him, she remained in place. "He did, but I need to hear you tell me. I want to understand why you are sacrificing everything."

"It's simple." Enrique rocked back on his heels. "I had a backup plan before I arrived in Gaullia. I did what needed to be done. Your happiness is paramount."

Madeleine came closer to him, cutting the distance between them in half. "What about your happiness?"

He avoided making eye contact. "I did what was necessary for both of us."

"So you don't want to marry me?" she asked.

He winced. "This is for the best."

Not caring that she was drawing attention from the staff, she placed her hands on her hips. "Why didn't I get a say in the matter?"

"You agreed to a marriage in name only last night," he said, his voice tight.

"I didn't have a say in that, either." Part of Madeleine wanted to fling her arms around him, but she was afraid. She might not be brave enough to have another relationship. But she would help Enrique understand he shouldn't decide what was best for theirs. "You gave me no choice. You offered no options. You can't do that when two people are involved, especially if you care about the other."

As his shoulders curled, he narrowed his eyes, brows squishing together. His mouth parted, but no words came out. He bit his lower lip before frowning. "The arrangement pleased you last night."

Her chest tightened. "I was in shock. What you said was unexpected. When I had time to think about the marriage you wanted, I wasn't okay. I barely slept."

Madeleine waited for him to say something, to reach out to her. But he didn't.

Had she misread him? Did he not care for her?

Madeleine inhaled, hoping to gather the strength to continue.

"I woke up expecting to get married, not to discover my life had been changed again without my having any say… Ever since Louie died, people have told me what I should do. About moving on and dating and everything else. None of which is their business. I'm tired of it." The words spewed out. "Yes, I was lost without Louie. I still grieve. I've never denied that, but I didn't lose my mind. I don't need someone else taking charge. I can make my own decisions and decide what's best for me."

Enrique's Adam's apple bobbed before he steeled his expression so no emotion showed. "My decision benefited you and your country. That is the only reason you agreed to the match—protection. Now, you no longer must marry to secure an alliance with Aliestle."

"What if I…" Her courage faltered.

She envied Jules and Izzy for being brave enough to go after what they'd wanted. Madeleine had only done that when she'd asked to attend graduate school, but that was for her self-preservation. She'd needed something else to focus on than only grief. Now, she wasn't sure how to proceed.

Unless she said something, nothing would change. Enrique would leave without her.

She wiped her clammy palms against her robe. "Tell me why you came to my room last night."

"I. Did." His words came out sharply. "I came to tell you the kind of marriage we should have."

"You were going to say something different," she countered. "You changed your mind. You were excited one moment and closed off the next. I assume you saw Louie's photo on my nightstand and his ring on my finger."

Enrique sighed, a heavy drawn out sound that appeared to drain his energy, given the way his shoulders dropped. "You love him."

"Yes, I do." She wasn't about to lie to him. "Nothing will change that. Except…"

He stared intently at her. "Except what?"

Her insides twitched. This was her chance to tell him. If she didn't, she would regret remaining silent forever.

Even though her mouth was Sahara dry, she swallowed. "I didn't think it was possible to love anyone else, but I was wrong. A heart is capable of loving more than one person. There is an infinite capacity of love. I learned that because of you."

He startled. "I…"

"I love you, Enrique."

There, she'd said it.

"I love you," Madeleine repeated in case she never had the opportunity to say that to him again. "I wanted—needed—you to know before you left."

Wide-eyed, he blinked rapidly. His chin jutted forward. "Louie—"

"Is dead," she interrupted. "I've been acting like I died with him, and a part of me did. I called him the love of my life, but that was only my first twenty-two years. Because of you, I'm happy I'm alive, and I'm ready to move forward with the love of the second part of my life. The one I want to start now. I hoped that would be with you, if you wanted me, but—"

"If I want you?" In the space of a heartbeat, Enrique bridged the distance between them. His expression was earnest. "I love you. You have no idea how much."

He loved her.

Madeleine's heart overflowed with love for this man. "Given you were willing to sacrifice your title and throne, I may have a slight idea."

"You were right about last night," he admitted. "I came to ask for a kiss. I couldn't tell you how I felt, not yet, so I figured that was second best. When I saw Louie's photo and his ring, I realized I couldn't compete with a ghost. You and I… We would both end up miserable. I couldn't do that to you, so I came up with the idea of a marriage in name only. But after I left your room, I realized I couldn't do that to myself, so I found another way to keep you and your country safe."

She didn't think it was possible, but her heart filled with more love for him. "By sacrificing everything you hold dear."

His gaze softened. "You're worth it."

Her toes curled. No hot kiss needed this time. "You said you want me to be happy."

He nodded.

"I'll be happiest with you by my side. I love you." She placed her hand over his heart, the way she'd done days ago. "I don't care if you're a crown prince. I just want to be with you. If you want to be with me."

He inhaled sharply before a smile brightened his face. "I do. More than anything. But I thought…"

"You were doing what I wanted."

Enrique nodded. "I've been selfish for so long I didn't want to make a mistake by putting myself first again."

She stared up at him through her eyelashes. "Next time, please don't assume what I want. Talk to me instead."

"I won't. And I will. Ask you, that is."

She forced herself not to hold her breath because she needed to ask. "Does that mean the wedding is back on?"

He dropped onto one knee and held her hand. "Will you marry me? Officially this time. No marriage contract is necessary."

Her pulse raced, matching her heart rate. "A real marriage?"

"One hundred percent real. Forget everything I said last night." Enrique kissed the top of her hand. "You hold my heart in your hands, my princess. You are my dream come true. The one who makes me believe a happily ever after is possible."

Flutters erupted in her stomach. Joy flowed through her. "Yes. I'll marry you."

Chapter Nineteen

e're getting married.

Anticipation and relief surged through Madeleine. And then reality hit. Getting married required a wedding. And her father had canceled theirs.

She grabbed Enrique's hand and pulled him inside. "My parents called off the wedding. I don't know if it's too late to say it's back on, but—"

He pulled her toward him and kissed her. Hard on the lips. "Go get ready. I'll take care of it."

"But no one is here." She bit her lip, mentally running over the list of what was supposed to be happening right now. "None of the hair or makeup or—"

Enrique kissed her again, making her mind go blank. He let go of her hand. "Trust me, my princess."

If heart-eyes existed, she had them. "I do."

His fingertips skimmed her jawline. "All that matters is if we can exchange vows and be pronounced husband and wife. It doesn't matter who is there or if it's at the cathedral."

True, except… "We need cake."

He laughed, a deep, rich sound she would happily grow old hearing. She couldn't wait.

"You shall have cake. Chocolate," Enrique declared. "If the baker has given away our original ones, I will bake you a wedding cake myself."

That she would like to see. She eyed him curiously. "Can you bake?"

"No, but there is a chef who can assist." He kissed her forehead. "Go to your room, so I can get busy."

She took a step toward the staircase and then turned. "I love you."

"I love you, too." He blew her a kiss.

In her bedroom, Madeleine went over a revised checklist—the most important things needing to be accomplished before getting married.

Hair.

Makeup.

Dress.

The massage, manicure, and food could wait. As

for photographs while she got ready, Lilia could take them. That reminded Madeleine. Had Enrique remembered they would need someone to photograph the wedding?

Her cell phone sat on her nightstand. She could text him.

No. He said to trust him.

I do.

She went into the bathroom and stared into the mirror. Talk about a bad hair day. She needed to shower again or plug in the straightener. She'd planned to wear an elaborate updo, but that wasn't a style she could pull off on her own. A basic French twist might work.

A knock sounded followed by a female voice. "Madeleine?"

She rushed out of the bedroom.

Jules and Izzy were there, each holding bags.

"Congratulations are in order." Jules's complexion glowed. "We're not professionals, but I've been known to style hair before."

Izzy stepped forward and hugged Madeleine. "Don't listen to her. The woman worked wonders with me. I was a grease monkey who didn't own a dress. You're already gorgeous and a proper princess. You'll be an exquisite bride by the time she's finished with you."

"Wait." Madeleine's gaze bounced between Jules and Izzy. "The two of you are helping me?"

Jules nodded. "Enrique called…"

"…And here we are," Izzy finished. "I'm not as skilled as our Jules, but I have learned a few tricks these past couple of years while wearing a tiara."

"Thank you." Madeleine didn't know what else to say.

Jules clapped her hands. "We don't have all day. It's time to transform you into a princess bride."

Madeleine pushed her shoulders back. "I'm ready."

"But your hair isn't quite there yet." Izzy covered her mouth with her hand. "Sorry, I didn't mean to say that aloud. That goes against the princess code."

Madeleine laughed. "You only said what I'm sure Jules thought. Because I did, too."

Jules shook her head. "We'll start with the unfortunate hair and go from there."

"I have a feeling I'm in good hands."

"The best." Izzy removed hair accessories and a curling wand. "A lot has happened in the past twelve hours or so. Focus on the good things. You can deal with the rest after your wedding day."

Madeleine's smile spread. Bliss flowed to the tips of her toes. "I will."

A few hours later, Enrique stood at the front of the cathedral with his brother on his left. He wore his country's uniform with a blue sash running across his chest.

His heart pounded. Not surprising, given what had happened since last night. But with help from his family, Brandt, Karl, Niko, and Jovan, the wedding was back on. The past few hours had been chaotic but worth it.

The opening chords from the organist played.

Enrique blew out a breath, focusing on the rear of the cathedral where his princess bride would enter. "This is it."

"I don't know how you pulled this off," Alejandro whispered in his ear. "Alaric appears to be in shock."

King Leon patted his brow with a handkerchief. He sat to the right, Gaullian tradition.

"So does my future father-in-law." Enrique kept his voice low.

"Well, I'm relieved because I didn't want to be king."

"You would have been a good one."

"You'll be better, bro."

Enrique's smile widened. "I will."

Alejandro laughed.

Enrique shot a glance his way. "It's true."

Alejandro held up his hands. "Not saying it isn't."

"We should have eloped. Or had the wedding on a ship like you and Jules did with only family and friends. Not every royal on the continent in attendance."

"Just remember, there will be cake later."

He nodded, grateful the baker hadn't disposed of their wedding cake yet. "Five flavors to choose from, since not everyone likes chocolate as much as Madeleine."

"And don't forget your wedding night."

Enrique's face heated. A real wedding meant a honeymoon. Best if he focused on the cake for now. No, his bride.

The doors of the church opened and Madeleine stood there, a vision in white.

Stunning.

He'd never seen anyone so gorgeous in his life.

Every nerve ending stood at attention. As she came closer, his pulse exploded, racing so fast he could barely breathe.

Alejandro nudged Enrique. Oh, right. He needed to move forward to meet his bride. His hands trembled.

Not from nerves but anticipation.

Okay, he was nervous, but only because he wanted the wedding to be perfect for her. And he wanted to be the man she believed him to be.

When she reached the front, Enrique laced his fingers with hers. With that one touch, his pulse settled. His nerves vanished.

She smiled at him.

The warmth in his heart spread through his veins, making its way through his entire body.

Every thought and emotion centered on this smart, caring, wonderful woman, who would soon be his wife.

Why did I think I could let her go? Walk away? Forget her?

He would never hide himself or how he felt. She would know she was his priority—his love.

"I love you, Mads," he whispered.

Her complexion glowed.

"It shall be my privilege to make you fall in love with me every single day for the rest of our lives," he added.

She squeezed his hand. "It'll be my privilege to let you do that. But I want my turn, too."

"Always, my princess."

His gaze met hers. The affection in her blue eyes took his breath away.

The bishop leaned forward. "Are you two finished so we can begin?"

Madeleine blushed, a charming shade of pink Enrique would be happy to see every single day for the rest of his life.

"We're just getting started, but go ahead." Enrique kissed the top of her hand. "We'll finish this later, my love."

Epilogue

Four months later…

Once upon a time, a young princess dreamed of marrying a crown prince and becoming his queen. As the years passed, parts of the dream changed. Not because she changed her mind, but because life had different plans in store for her. She experienced happiness, love, tears, heartache, sorrow, love again, and then joy.

So much joy.

Overflowing in a way she couldn't have imagined

five years ago when loss darkened her world and withered her heart.

But somehow in doing what was expected, in putting royal duty ahead of her own desires, she found something special, something unexpected.

Love.

Enrique wasn't the crown prince who'd starred in her teenaged dreams, but he was the man she loved— her husband and the future father of their children. The past four months had been a dream come true. Oh, there were mishaps, but this was real life, not a fairy tale. Still each day was better than the last.

Madeleine had believed her ability to love died with Louie. She'd been oh so wrong. Between that first awkward meeting with Enrique and their wedding day, she'd fallen for him. Fallen hard.

He wasn't perfect, but he was perfect for her.

Their love grew each day. When they were apart, she counted the days until they would be together again.

Love.

Unconditional love.

Her affection for Enrique hadn't replaced her feelings for Louie. He would always be in her heart, as would Enrique.

Only in different ways.

And that was…okay.

There was room enough for both of them. As she'd told Enrique, the heart had an infinite amount of love to give. That was something she hadn't understood until Enrique entered her life.

The beautiful orchestra music filled the cathedral on La Isla de la Aurora. Goose bumps covered Madeleine's skin. The percussionist's pounding on the timpani matched the beat of her heart.

As she glanced at Enrique, who sat next to her, warmth radiated through Madeleine.

Love had prevailed.

Love had banished the darkness.

Today, on Coronation Day, there was only light.

The same as when she'd married her husband in Gaullia's cathedral four months ago. Although, truthfully, that was the case from their first walk at the castle.

Enrique rested his hand on top of hers. His skin was warm yet rough because of the calluses from working in his garden. His touch reaffirmed they were in this together.

Not that there was another way.

Each were better—stronger—with the other at their side.

Someone coughed. One of the many times given the pews were filled with diplomats, royals, and a few lucky ticket-holders through a national lottery.

Not that anyone would miss a second.

A cable news network positioned cameras to capture each moment for the viewers at home. Outside the cathedral, crowds lined the streets, listening to the audio feed and watching the streaming of the coronation.

Enrique's family was participating in the ceremony and was seated nearby. Her parents and Karl sat in the front pew near the robed members of Parliament, who were as stuffy as she imagined they would be. Several wore frowns because their plans to keep one of King Dario's sons from the throne failed.

King Dmitar, Queen Beatrice, Prince Niko, and Princess Izzy sat behind them. King Alaric, his wife, and four sons, including Brandt, were in a pew across the aisle.

The archbishop prayed before anointing Enrique with the sacred oil and then did the same to Madeleine.

She preferred this fragrance to the incense used earlier, but both smells would be burned into her memory.

Madeleine wanted to capture each scent and sound so she could tell their children and grandchildren about this. Those details would make the video seem real. One of those young ones listening in the future would go through this same ceremony someday.

As the archbishop recited the royal oath to Enrique, her pulse kicked up.

Enrique raised his chin. "I do solemnly promise."

Pride flowed through her. He'd been king for the past month and a half, but the coronation marked the official beginning of his reign.

As the archbishop placed a crown on his head and

a gold scepter in his right hand, tears blurred Madeleine's vision.

This was Enrique's dream—one he'd been willing to give up for her. Thank goodness, she'd admitted her true feelings before it was too late.

Coronets sounded.

And then, it was her turn.

The many rehearsals had made her actions and words rote. She straightened.

The archbishop spoke the royal oath of the queen consort.

Her heart pounded. Nerve endings tingled.

This was it.

Her entire life, she'd prepared and trained for this moment.

A quick glance at Enrique, seeing his warm smile and love-filled gaze, settled her nerves.

She inhaled. "I do solemnly promise."

The archbishop placed a crown on her head. Heavy and uncomfortable, but this was the price to be paid.

More coronets sounded. The archbishop spoke other words and offered a blessing. And then the ceremony was over.

Procession music played. That was the signal to proceed up the aisle. Each step took forever. On either side of the aisle, smiling faces offered their congratulations. The chant of "Long live King Enrique" sounded from outside.

All she wanted was to hold Enrique's hand, but

that wasn't allowed. Instead, she waved to those she knew and those she didn't.

As they stepped outside, a deafening cheer erupted from the crowd. She waved to them, too.

Now that they were no longer in the cathedral, Enrique laced his fingers with hers. "The crown suits you."

"As does yours." She squeezed his hand. "Congratulations, Your Majesty."

He kissed the top of her hand. "Thank you, Your Majesty."

The coronation's event planner motioned to the horse-drawn royal carriage waiting for them. "This way, Your Majesties."

The four splendid white horses stood patiently, not the slightest bit nervous from the large crowd. Gold ribbons were braided in their manes. Even their harnesses were decorated.

A uniformed footman helped Madeleine into the carriage. Enrique followed and sat next to her. He held her hand.

A sense of peace washed over her.

The titles and crowns would enable them to leave a legacy, but all she needed was him.

A band, marching guards, and soldiers on horseback led the coronation procession to the palace. People, five-deep in places, lined the streets. She waved again and received delighted smiles in return. "A big crowd came out to see you today."

"See *us*." Enrique's smile sent tingles shooting through her. "This is the first coronation in nearly fifty years, so it's a big deal."

"I pray there isn't another for fifty or sixty more."

He kissed her hand again. That was easier than trying to negotiate with the heavy crowns on their heads. "From your mouth to God's ears."

When the carriage reached the palace, Ortiz escorted them inside and removed their crowns. Madeleine felt ten pounds lighter, which she was. He handed her two ibuprofen tablets and a glass of water. "Take these to ward off a headache."

She did. "Thank you."

The man had worked for the royal family for decades. He'd made her feel welcome the instant she'd arrived after their honeymoon cruise on a private yacht, courtesy of King Alaric. The tyrant appeared to have a softer side he rarely showed.

Ortiz glanced at a schedule. "You have thirty minutes before the reception begins, Your Majesties."

"Thank you, Ortiz," Enrique said. "We will be ready."

"Time for a catnap?" Madeleine asked.

"I have something to show you first."

Holding her hand, he led her toward the garden he loved so much. A briny breeze blew, the scents of salt and flowers tickling her nose.

"Close your eyes," he said.

"What—?"

"Please."

She did as told.

"It isn't far," he said.

Madeleine took a hesitant step. "Where are we going?"

"You'll see soon enough." His tone held a hint of mystery. He placed his hand at her lower back. "It's a surprise."

Madeleine inhaled sharply. "You're not one for surprises."

"That's because I worry I'll mess up. But I've been doing better."

"You have." She had a feeling if she could see his face he was beaming.

"I hope I haven't made a mistake with this one."

"I'm sure it's wonderful." She would love anything he did for her. "Are we there yet?"

He laughed. "Is my proper princess impatient?"

"Yes. But I'm an impatient queen now," she teased.

"My apologies, Your Majesty."

"How much longer?" she asked, curious.

"We're almost there."

Flowing water sounded. Not the waves against the shore. This was different. More consistent with a pattern.

"You can stop." He placed his hands on her shoulders. "Open your eyes."

She did.

Madeleine stood in front of a large fountain. Water shot thirty feet in the air and then cascaded down the tiered bowls. She did a double take.

Her heart lodged in her throat. She swallowed. "Is it…?"

"A few pieces are from Louie's fountain in Gaullia. The person I hired could never get it to work properly. I couldn't move all the fountain, so I had a new one designed using the pieces we could bring to the island. So some parts are from Louie and others from me. Together, they make a whole fountain for you. One that finally works, my love."

She threw her arms around Enrique. "Thank you. This is the best surprise. I love it. And I love you."

He pulled her against him. "I love you."

A closer look showed Madeleine what he'd given up to do this for her. "You tore out part of your garden so the fountain would fit."

"Our garden." His gaze seemed to see her inner soul. "I wanted you to have something from home and from Louie besides his photograph and ring."

"I couldn't ask for anything more."

Enrique kissed her, a kiss that shouted his love for her and hinted at their future—however long that might last. Because she would never take their time together for granted.

Not one minute.

She'd found love again with this man—this king—who held her in his arms and pressed his lips against hers. She had no idea how or if happily ever after would beat this moment—or any of the others they'd shared—but she couldn't wait to find out.

About the Author

USA Today bestselling author Melissa McClone has written over forty-five sweet contemporary romance novels. She lives in the Pacific Northwest with her husband, three children, two spoiled Norwegian Elkhounds, and cats who think they rule the house. They do!

If you'd like to find Melissa online:
www.melissamcclone.com
www.facebook.com/melissamcclonebooks
www.facebook.com/groups/McCloneTroopers
twitter.com/melissamcclone
www.instagram.com/melmcclone

Other Books by Melissa McClone

STANDALONE

A matchmaking aunt wants her nephew
to find love under the mistletoe…
The Christmas Window

SERIES
All series stories are standalone,
but past characters may reappear.

The Billionaires of Silicon Forest
Who will be the last single man standing?
The Wife Finder
The Wish Maker
The Deal Breaker

Quinn Valley Ranch
Relatives in a large family find love in Quinn Valley, Idaho…
Carter's Cowgirl
Summer Serenade

Beach Brides and Indigo Bay Sweet Romance Series
A mini-series within two multi-author series…
Jenny
Sweet Holiday Wishes
Sweet Beginnings

Her Royal Duty
Royal romances with charming princes and dreamy castles...
The Accidental Princess
The Reluctant Princess
The Not-So-Perfect Princess
The Proper Princess

THE PROPER PRINCESS

One Night to Forever Series
Can one night change your life...and your relationship status?
Fiancé for the Night
The Wedding Lullaby
A Little Bit Engaged
Love on the Slopes
The One Night To Forever Box Set: Books 1-4

Mountain Rescue Series
Finding love in Hood Hamlet with a
little help from Christmas magic...
His Christmas Wish
Her Christmas Secret
Her Christmas Kiss
His Second Chance
His Christmas Family

Ever After Series
Happily ever after reality TV style...
The Honeymoon Prize
The Cinderella Princess
Christmas in the Castle

Love at the Chocolate Shop Series
Three siblings find love thanks to
Copper Mountain Chocolate...
A Thankful Heart
The Valentine Quest
The Chocolate Touch

The Bar V5 Ranch Series
Fall in love at a dude ranch in Montana...
Home for Christmas
Mistletoe Magic
Kiss Me, Cowboy
Mistletoe Wedding
A Christmas Homecoming

www.ingramcontent.com/pod-product-compliance
Lightning Source LLC
Chambersburg PA
CBHW050339190726
48284CB00007BB/2068